THE

WAY

THE

LIGHT

BENDS

Cordelia Jensen

Philomel Books

Also by Cordelia Jensen

Skyscraping

PHILOMEL BOOKS
an imprint of Penguin Random House LLC
375 Hudson Street, New York, NY 10014

Philomel Books is a registered trademark of Penguin Random House LLC.

Library of Congress Cataloging-in-Publication Data
Names: Jensen, Cordelia, author. | Title: The way the light bends / Cordelia
Jensen. | Description: New York, NY : Philomel Books, [2018]
Summary: Although best friends as children, Linc and her adopted sister
have drifted apart as Holly excels at school, sports, and pleasing their
mother, while Linc struggles academically and yearns to be a photographer. |
Identifiers: LCCN 2017029204 | ISBN 9780399547447 (hardcover) |
ISBN 9780399547461 (e-book) | Subjects: | CYAC: Novels in verse. |
Sisters—Fiction. | Individuality—Fiction. | Photography—Fiction. |
Dating (Social customs)—Fiction. | Family life—New York (State)—
New York—Fiction. | New York (N.Y.)—Fiction. |
Classification: LCC PZ7.5.J46 Way 2018 | DDC [Fic]—dc23 |
LC record available at https://lccn.loc.gov/2017029204
Printed in the United States of America.
ISBN 9780399547447
10 9 8 7 6 5 4 3 2 1

Edited by Liza Kaplan. Design by Jennifer Chung.
Text set in Adobe Jenson Pro.

For every teen who has struggled with self-esteem
and made choices—at times—that reflect this struggle,

I see you.

I believe in you.

In destruction, there is creation.

Reservoir

Reservoir

CAPTURING

WHAT'S ALIVE

With a click
and a breath

I capture branches
        squirrels
        pigeons

        two girls
            skipping
            in time
everything alive, pulsing—
the park
the heartbeat of Manhattan,
            of who we used to be.

Holly doesn't notice
the beauty in
            the shape of a puddle
            the curved blade of grass,
doesn't remember
        jogs right by
            the trickling stream that
            became rushing water when our wands
            commanded.
        Too focused on her boyfriend Stefano
            on school
            on soccer
        for any memory of us.

I take picture after picture
        till I'm so   far behind
I'm not sure I can catch up.

3

IN RHYTHM

We used to be
    two girls
        walking
        hand in hand
        arms wrapped around each other
                                  tight

her hand deep brown,
mine freckly, white,
matching steps and skips
our footsteps falling in rhythm

two beams of light
two stretching shadows

moving side by side

    in tempo
    in time.

TOGETHER, APART

Now we are
      two girls
      walking
through Central Park
      //together, apart//

one

      hands wrapped tight around
      my camera, my phone

the other

      hands wrapped tight around
      someone else

t   p
w   a
o   t
      h
       s

      one in light
      one in shadow

diverging.

PEER THROUGH

Finally,
we stop in front of our brownstone.

Being on academic probation
means going
straight home
after school.
Our parents text,
            check in with me,
                        with Holly,
make sure I'm following
                        their command.

Today
I have no choice.

        But if Holly wasn't here,   if Stefano wasn't here,

                        I would walk

                                                straight past
                        the house
                turn down the street
                peer through the window
                        of the Westside Center for
                        the Arts—

                with only
                        the wind
                        watching.

BETWEEN US

Instead,
Holly & I walk
through the gate together
             us two.

But even   as we do
        her Greek prince
          comes between us
      grabs her brown hand
      with his beige one.

The bird carved into
the side of our steps
frowns a little.

We used to play
the prince slept
while the princesses
ruled the land.

Now Stefano takes Holly's key
      opens the door
like it's his own.

Once we were Linc & Holly
        trading snow cones
        chasing squirrels
        wearing matching sandals.

But now,
it's Holly & Stefano
                          Linc.

THROUGH THE DOOR

Holly & Stefano rush past me
they   know Mom & Dad aren't home
they   close themselves in her room.

I turn the volume up
on my talk show.
Three loud women squawk at each other.

Open my chemistry textbook.

> *Elements that belong to the same group*
> *usually show chemical similarities.*

As the women interrupt each other,
I write down the rule.

My pencil lingers over the words

belong

group

and

usually.

SHIELDING

Once upon a time,
    sixth grade,

    Holly would help me
    with my homework.
    I would help her
        decorate her room,
        or let her score goals on me,
        or teach her a new drawing technique.

    We'd make deals.

    "I'll help you with your science project
    if you help with mine for art."

One day,
a guy named Gabe
asked Holly to the movies.
Mom would only let her go
if there was a group.

Holly got Gabe
to ask Max
to take me
    lent me her
sweater,
lip gloss,
boots.

I didn't want to go
but I owed her—
she'd helped me with my math all morning.

Gabe & Holly
held hands, giggled,
played in the arcade
        beforehand.
Max never looked my way,
spent the whole time
on his phone.

        On the way out of the movies,
        I tripped, spilled soda
        on the sweater, boots.

Max just laughed.

When I asked for his napkin,
he told me to get one
myself.
Called me
an idiot.

When Mom asked
what happened to the sweater,
Holly did what she often did:

        ~~~lied~~~ for me.

Said it was her fault, an accident.

Later,
we sat in her room,
curled knees touching.
She was so angry at Max,
said we should get him back.

Said she wasn't going to let anyone   ignore, tease
    me.

My heart swelled
with love for Holly.

Once upon a time,

    we were
    princesses
        making deals
        casting spells
        facing the world
    together.

Once upon a time.

UNEVEN

Dad comes home
        blue button-down shirt, rolled at the sleeve
        wrinkled around the collar
        glasses uneven.

He leans his light arm
on the navy chair in the den
that no one ever sits in.

In my mind,
I take a photo
of the colors
contrasted,
        then switch them.
Him blue,
chair white.

"Chemistry, huh?"
he says,
turns off the TV,
asks if he can help.

I look down at my notes,
                my drawings,
shrug.

"You hungry?
How about an apple?
Brain food,"
        he says.

As he goes to the fridge,

I text Holly.

Dad's home.

She doesn't text back but
minutes later
        they appear together—
        Holly with a new outfit on.
        Stefano all smiles.

VERTEBRAE TO VERTEBRAE

An hour later,
    Stefano gone
    Holly out for a run
    Dad cooking,
    me still struggling with the same assignment.

Mom enters—6:35 p.m. sharp.
    Hangs up her key
        on the hook labeled "Mom."
    Walks to the sink.
    Washes her hands.

Dad stirs soup, kisses her cheek.
Holly walks in, sweaty,
greets her in the kitchen.

They open 3 seltzers
    pop
    pop
    pop.

I close chemistry. Unfinished.
Move on to math.

I watch them all,
    listen in
from my spot in the living room.

Holly tells Mom
she
    is running for student council

got moved up to advanced math
is trying for starting goalie.

Mom tells Holly
about work:
    "a particularly complex
    spinal surgery."

Reconnecting   vertebrae   to   vertebrae.

Dad smiles at them both.

They don't look anything alike
        Holly, black
        Mom, white
but
standing tall
their backbones both
link
success
to
success
to
success.

CALCULATIONS

Mom yells to me from the kitchen:
　　　"Linc, honey, how was your day?"

I look down.
Instead of finding
the surface area
of a cylinder
I've colored it in.

"Fine," I say.

　　　"Any details you care to share?"

Sure. I could tell her:
　　　I failed a pop quiz in chem.
　　　My history teacher's the hardest one in the school.
　　　Ellery's parents are letting her take an art elective.

But before I can answer
　　　she sighs deeply
　　　mutters something
and then she says louder:
　　　"Did you hear all of Holly's exciting news?"

So I erase the cylinder.
Shade it back in.
Listen to Mom & Holly calculate
strategies for success.
I
　　　　　fill.
And
then　　　　　　　　　erase.

COURAGE

Once—
in eighth grade,
I got up the courage,
        asked Dad why

            Mom

        liked Holly better.

He said, "Don't be
ridiculous."

But then
he saw how
upset I was.

                        A siren wailed. A dog barked.

        He sat me down

told me how

        when the adoption went through
        Mom read everything she could
        about how to be a good mother
        to an adopted child.
        She studied like she was
        in med school
        again.

        Mom was determined
        to make up for the fact
        that her and Holly's DNA

17

didn't match.
That they would never
look like each other.

But it was different with me.
I was her biological child.

"So what about for me?
What did she do when she found out about me?"
Dad looked at me closely.

A kid cried. A taxi honked.
"She was very excited,"
he said,
and smiled.

It didn't really

answer

my question

but I never had the courage to ask it

again.

TWO ROUTES

I.

We are twins
(virtual ones)
Holly only four months older,
adopted from Ghana   at six months old.

Mom volunteered there
after med school,
doctoring orphaned children.

She knew then

as she bandaged
and vaccinated

she'd return someday

to mother a Ghanaian child
of her own.

The adoption was already set
when they found out:

she was pregnant.

II.

Once I asked
if I was an accident,

Dad smiled, said no—
a marvelous surprise.

III.

Holly & I
used to pretend
we were named after
the New York tunnels

      Holland & Lincoln
two routes to the same city.

We would lie down

/side by side/

pretend
to let the world
rush through us,
reach our arms overhead,
tip our fingers
to lightly touch,
our point of convergence.

IV.

Now,
when Mom's disappointment in me
      stains our walls,
when it drowns
      out the street noise,
when it cracks
      over my skin,

I want to remind her
      I'm the one
she carried in her belly.

OVERLAP

Mom
only sees Holly & me
in opposition.

>   Holly: hardworking.
>   Linc: careless.

>   Holly: bright.
>   Linc: dim.

She spits my name—

Linc

says hers
pigeon-coo soft—

Holly.

And each time
my stomach sinks

wondering if I might ever
be enough—
whether Mom might ever
see where we overlap—

whether she might ever

speak my name
—gently—
like hers.

HOVERING

From my room,
I can hear Holly down the hall
        chatting with her best friend Maggs.
Saying something about Stefano
and Saturday.
After she hangs up,
like clockwork
        9:45 p.m.
Mom comes into her room
to go over the next day's schedule.

Ellery texts me an image:
        half her big toe
        hovering above a blue blanket.

                    We play a game
                    where we send
                        drawings
                        photos
            and the other person creates
                    a caption for the image.

So I write:
        Moon over water.
She texts back a thumbs-up.

My turn:
                On my wall, I sketch monster teeth
            on a cartoon bunny.
                Take a photo.
Her turn to give my image a name.

MORE/LESS

Once Mom's done with Holly,
she enters my room,
    scans over all my homework,
    makes sure I've finished it all.

She picks up my notebooks,
without asking.
Rubs her temples,
leafs through notes for geometry,
sighs at chemistry.

    "Linc, let's try to start sophomore year off differently.
    More learning, less doodling, okay?
    You'll need to work much harder to get off probation."

She lays my notebook down.

Ellery texts back: **Rabid rabbit.**

I can't help but smile.
Mom thinks I'm laughing at her.
Her voice changes
to the one Holly & I used to call
"Mean Queen," says:

    "There's nothing funny about failure."

Closes the door
behind her as she leaves.
I never even got
a chance to speak.

ART FOR SCIENTISTS

Lying on my bed, keep drawing on my wall.

      I fill in the bunny's ears.
      Give him a field to play in.

Then, lie back,
remember how
      once upon   a long time ago
      Mom was impressed
by my art
  my creativity.

She bought me
my first set of
watercolors, brushes.

Used to laugh, say
      "how fascinating"
she ended up with a child
          who was an artist
when she could only draw
stick figures.

Sometimes, we'd all play school,
         me the art teacher,
         Holly teaching science,
         Mom & Dad, the students.

No matter how hard Mom tried to draw a face,
the features would come out

//lopsided
//uneven.

No matter how hard Mom tried to instill in me
her love of science and math, of school,
        fractions

                swirled &
                        fell
        shapes
    overshadowed
        theories.

Through colors & images I could always
say more
than with words & numbers.

        Once upon   a long time ago

she bought me
my first set of
watercolors, brushes.

But now,
my art is

"just

a distraction."

SPELL CASTING

I.
Freshman year
Photo 1—
Mom let me take
an elective.

I met a girl
who wore a shirt
with an embroidered fuchsia Pegasus.

Her parents
insisted she go to Ketchum
after years of homeschooling
even though she hated
math & science
(just like I did).

She said she liked
my lime-green boots.
"I'm Ellery, by the way."

And in that first moment
I couldn't help but wonder—
could we be the same?

II.
As the year went on,
Ellery switched into 3D Art.

I stuck with photography.
Knew
                I was meant

to do more than just
capture a moment—
I was meant to
give the invisible   visibility.
I created my own reality
in the digital darkroom
(cutting, transforming, color adjusting, cropping, sharpening),
watching my world come alive.

THE DIFFERENCES BETWEEN

It turns out
the differences
between Ellery & me
go beyond art preference:

>Her parents,
>owners of the Müller Gallery,
>let her take art again this year,
>they always //encourage// her to
>explore her creativity.

>She never seems to study,
>but she never
>seems to fail.

My parents
insist the reason
my GPA slipped below 2.0
last year
was because of my obsession

>with my camera,
>with my art.

That I did murals instead of math problems,
compositions instead of calculations.

Now,
I have weekly meetings with my advisor,
weekly reports from my teachers.

Every adult
holds me in their focus,
ready to capture
a negative image
of me.

If only
I were graded
in photography
on artistic merit
I know I could be like Holly
getting

A's.
A's.
A's.

LOST TRACK

Next morning, on the way to school,
I snap photos
    a bird's wing,
    an open window,
    feet walking.

Holly is tense,
        cracks her neck, flicks her wrist,
        blinks her eyes too many times.
      "Did you vote for me?" she asks
as we walk to the bus.

A thunderbolt crashes into my gut.

I consider lying.

But maybe the truth doesn't matter?
Maybe she doesn't really need my vote?

"I forgot," I admit.
"I meant to
        but Ellery showed me her new art project—
          we totally   lost track of time."

Holly's lips move side to side

      then—
she picks up the pace.
To show she's mad.

Crash.
Boom.

SIDELINES

Maggs is already at the bus stop.
We board.

Maggs, mixed race,
her skin's closer to Holly's color
than mine.

Looking at us
side by side by side,
you'd see a rainbow.

But—they are part of something
I am not.

They're busy
talking dresses
for some athlete-scholar luncheon.

       Holly, an academic scholar.
       Linc, on academic probation.

"You could wear that coral one,"
I offer.

       Holly shoots me a look.
       "I outgrew it a long time ago."

I watch the park wind past me.

They move on to soccer.
Holly's chances
of playing starting goalie.

I picture her
in the goal zone
making save
after save
after save.

       Holly, goal-oriented.
       Linc, without aim.

Me, on the sidelines,
taking pictures of the grass

how it moves in the wind like waves.

CARRIAGES

The bus crosses east through Central Park.
I look to the leaves
   snap shots of the tunnels
   the paths that lead
   back west—
remember—

when we were eight, Dad brought
Holly and me to an exhibition
on the creation of the park.

He's a historian,
knows all about the city's past.

Holly & I became entranced
by the fashion of old New York,
the maps of Seneca Village—
                the village that existed
                    1825–1857
                before the Park was a park.
One map showed where African Americans,
Irish and German immigrants lived—
        their   schools
                churches
                water sources
juxtaposed with a map of the city now.

We realized
how close we lived
to where the village used to be.
In our minds
we could see people

raising goats in the park.
Washing their clothes
in the stream.

For months after, we played
"Saving Seneca Village."
Holly was Catherine,
the African American schoolteacher,
I was Mary, an Irish girl
who begged to join Colored School Number 3.

I was always misbehaving in class,
she was always writing down the rules.

The end of the play
was always the same:
Catherine & Mary fought the wealthy buyers
and Central Park was never built,
the village stood strong,
just where it was always
meant to be.

I still go to the stream sometimes
            the stream that saw the village become the park
                now called Tanner's Spring
and picture people there,

their   homes,
            goats,
            laundry lines.

But without Holly
it's only half a history.

DIMLY LIT

Off the bus,
  walking ahead of me
        Maggs & Holly
            swat each other
                laugh
                    share earbuds
                        take selfies.

Ellery
        with her long, blond, tangled hair,
        rosy white skin,
        purple cowboy boots,
        "That's a Wrap!" T-shirt
greets me at the
        school's main entrance
hands me a donut.
Sprinkled.

Asks do I want to
                        //cut//
first period.

"Hello? Probation?" I say.

We walk inside.
Follow her ~~~~~~~~

        the only **bright light**
        sparkling through
        the dimly lit hall.

DAYDREAM

In chemistry
Mr. Torres talks about the
periodic table
      but all I see is a staircase.

            Skeletons
            marching

up

down

over

        elements //without// groups
        surrounded by things that don't
        belong.

COLLAPSING SAILS

In third grade,
I stood outside a therapist's office,
    listened as the doctor gave Mom
a "diagnosis":

            "overactive imagination."

        "That's it?"
            I could hear her through the door.
        "Not ADD?"

I watched

            the curtains on the windows
                            fly up
to meet each other, like sails.

        "Well, we'll have to get a tutor,"
                            she told my dad.

A few years later,
she decided
tutors were a waste of money.

        "I just don't see any improvement . . ."
                    She would sigh, scratch her head
                    as if I was
                    a problem she couldn't quite solve.

By sixth grade she'd chalked it up to
laziness, carelessness.

A downed sail that
no one was strong enough
to lift back up again.

Made me promise to work harder
"like Holly,"
she said,
ignoring the true diagnosis:
that I would never be like her.

DESTRUCTION

In seventh grade,
    after failing my science project,
    after constant comparisons by teachers,

        Holly, excellent
        Linc, struggling

I stole Holly's work.

Carried her poster to my room.

Couldn't hear
again
    how hard she'd worked,
    how well she'd done.

She walked in on me
destroying her project
drawing over
her big, red
    A+
with a big, black
Sharpie.

Holly screamed
until Mom came running
in too.

When I was done,
only five words
still legible on her poster:
    The truth of our DNA.

PROTECTION

Once I was caught,
Holly yelled, "No more!"

I knew she meant:

> No more helping me with my homework.
> No more borrowing sweaters.
> No more getting Mom to go easy on me.

As Holly cried, Mom held her, wiped her tears.

Mom yelled too,
said I *could not,*
    should not
take out my own failing
on my sister.

I was grounded
for a month.

Before I went to my room
I heard Mom whisper to Holly
she would never let me
hurt her again.

She was there to protect her.

Suddenly I was someone
    my sister
    my twin
needed protection from.

ROSES & THORNS

It was then that
what had been Holly & me

became
Holly & Mom.

There was no more Mean Queen.
     Just one sweet princess
     and one evil one.

Just two roses
and me, the thorn
with a briar
//grown thick//
between us.

ENOUGH CHANGE

At the start of Ketchum,
        Mom relieved when I got in,
        happy for a while when I did,
                Holly & I had a
                new school
                new beginning
                        together
the briar thinned out.

The week before,
we even went school shopping
        just us two
        practiced our new commute.

But the school year began—
Holly quickly found her group
and I found Ellery.

There was enough change
//to cut through//
the briar,
enough for us to
~~peek back in~~

at each other.
But not enough
for us to find
each other's hands
                                and hold on.

SNAP & CLICK

Ellery & I eat lunch
with the other kids
who don't fit in.

   People stuck in the wrong picture.

I watch Holly & Stefano
sitting so close,
his tongue almost
down her throat.
She's barely spoken to me
since I told her I forgot to vote.

When she gets up
to get a drink,
he chucks some trash
at a freshman's tray.

Holly insists:
He's handsome
smart
athletic and
        amazingly
also <u>kind</u>.

She doesn't see
how he acts differently
when she's not there.

        I've tried to tell her I don't trust him but
        she doesn't seem to mind.
Ellery follows my gaze

shakes her head.
        Knowing I think Stefano's a jerk.
        Knowing I think Holly deserves better.

"No way they'll last forever,"
        she says.
I feel a lump rise in my throat.
Then she says what I can't,
"But she'll <u>always</u> be your sister."

I feel the lump grow
bigger.
I want to say
I hope that's true.
Instead I change the subject,
ask Ellery about her project.

Before she can answer
the bell rings,
lunch is over.
"Talk later?"

I nod, watch
as Ellery goes to art
as Holly goes the other way—
as "kind" Stefano slaps a freshman on the head,
                                passes by me
                without even saying hi.

With just a snap & a click
I capture him,
then Photoshop him
right
out.

TRANSPORT

I walk to Mr. Chapman's office.
Weekly meeting with my advisor.
He used to be an engineer
but now he sits
                constructing words
                shaping them
into unfortunate news.

When he sees me,
he waves me in.

        "Sit down, Ms. Malone."

I do.

        "So, we're a month into the school year, and I'm not hearing
        great things from your science teacher so far.
        Or from math.
        Being on academic probation means you need
        a C or above in each class.
        Your English grade is the strongest, a solid B.
        From these reports, it seems like you are managing a 2.4,
        but—

        There's little room for error. Capiche?"

He balances a pencil
on a mug.

Then, as usual:
        "So many kids would love to have your spot, Linc.
        I'd hate to see you waste this opportunity."

"What about the B in English? Pretty good!"
I pretend to be cheery.

      He just looks at me,
      frowns.

I tell him I'll do better,
but we both know
that's not true.

Some people are good
students,
some aren't.

I turn the knob
on the door,
feel it
transport me
someplace else.

THE LONG WAY HOME

Alone, I
take the long way home from school.
Try to push Mr. Chapman's words down.

          Peer in the window of the
Westside Center for the Arts.
     The scanners,
     the printers,
     the easels.

This time though, I'm spotted.
The door opens.

     "Can I help you?"
     asks a woman.

I pause.
When Holly & I were young,
I was always the one brave enough to

Take. The. Dare.
          One deep breath and go:
"Do you have photography classes?"

Her face lights up,
tells me to come inside.
The woman hands me class brochures
     digital,
     landscape,
     black & white.

"You can register online or use this form."

Maybe my parents would let me
take a Saturday class
if I got the bulk of my homework done on Friday?
Glance at the class prices.
I could offer to pay for half?

Walking home,
I focus on
the way the sun
lights up
the reddening leaves
sparked

bright   and changing.

BALANCING

Home to a quiet house,
Holly at soccer practice,

I try to balance formulas.

I hear the
door open,
then close.

Before I even say hello
I hand him
the brochure.

"Just Saturdays? Please? I know it's expensive
but I could use my allowance for some
and pay the rest back."

Dad shifts his weight.
Foot to foot.

He smiles, then sighs,
says we'll talk about it
when Mom gets home.

PRIORITIES

Later, she enters in her scrubs, eyes puffy.

       Dad brings her up to speed.

She says this is only the beginning of the year.
My grades need to be top priority.

       "But what if I did all my homework on Fridays.
       Work really hard.
       Get off academic probation?"

Mom shakes her head, yawning,
"You should be trying to get off probation, class or no class."

       "Dad?"

              "We're just asking that you try to make academics
              your focus, honey. Get through this rough patch,"
                           he says, pouring Mom some tea.

As always,
       their message is the same:
       art, photography
       pull me out
                          away

from what's important—

How can I make them see
       they are the only things
that pull me back in?

PLAYING ALONG

Mom heads upstairs
as I page through
description after description
of classes
I'll never be allowed to take.

When Holly gets home,
she eyes my brochure.

"Are they going to let you take a class?"

I shake my head no,
surprised she's decided to speak to me.

"Those pictures you took last year?"

> (One of Holly running, fists to the sky)
>> (Another, Ellery, painting her shoe)
>>> (An iced-over stream upstate in winter)

"They were good."
She stretches,
limbs long and lean.

Warmth radiates through me.
I tell her thanks.

"Hey, congratulations on the election, by the way.
Sorry again I forgot to vote."

She turns her head to me then,
her straightened hair flopping over to the side,
says it's okay
and gives me half a smile.

My mind freezes the moment,
frames her face
in a picture.

STATUES

People always looked at us   //always//
when we were little.
We tried to laugh them off,

play "museum"
                                   //pretend//
freeze-frame.

We were   statues.
           On display.

I'd yell:
"She's my sister! We're twins!"

Holly would giggle.
Grab my hand.

Mom would try to shush me up.
Embarrassed by the   //attention.//

But Holly would turn to me anyway.
We'd make our "identical face,"
the one where we rolled our eyes back,
stuck our tongues out to the side.

"Don't we look alike now?" she'd say, laughing.

"Can't you tell we're twins?" I'd giggle.

As we got older
people no longer stared
but I would still

yell out
anyway,
"We're sisters!"

Holly would shush me,

                                            //look away//

as if by turning her head
she could pretend
all the questions weren't there,
make them disappear.

And my heart became a statue then.

Wondering   //if she wished//
I would vanish too.

IMAGINE ANYTHING

In the kitchen
I hear Mom
        celebrating Holly's student council win,
        asking about her soccer practice,
        discussing dominant and recessive genes.

I go to my room,
click into the Westside Center for the Arts website.
                Look at student work.

Scroll down to "Events."
        The Center has a gallery showcasing
        not just Westside student work
        but prominent neighborhood artists'
        work from NYC-based art schools.

Saturday, 8 p.m.
Innovative Arts Academy
student showcase

I click the link.

Words flash:
Innovative Arts Academy
            Where We Are Artists First.
                    Imagine Anything.
                    Then Make It Real.

My heart clicks like a roller-coaster car,
going up
            up
                up.

INNOVATION

That night, Mom spot-checks my homework,
says she's glad I answered every chem question
but some of them look incorrect.
Tells me to double-check
            redo my work.

When she leaves,
I click back into IAA's website.

> Photo 1: four kids collaborating on a hallway mural.
> Photo 2: a green-haired girl taking a close-up of a violet.
> Photo 3: kids in red-and-white-striped costumes bowing
> on a stage.

Is this really a school?

Click on *Admissions*.

```
To apply:
GPA requirements           2.7 preferred
                           (exceptions
                           made for
                           outstanding
                           portfolios)
Teacher Recommendation     Art teacher
                           preferred
Artist Portfolio           12 complete,
                           thematically
                           connected pieces
Application deadline       11/15 for
                           following fall
                           semester start
```

Less than two months from now.

And then
          below
I see:

Applicants must write an Artist's
Statement.

What is your vision?
What truth are you trying to capture with
your art?

Colors brighten.
My mind spins.

I look back at the IAA students,

see myself
next to the green-haired girl,
with my own camera
taking close-ups
of the petals' shadows.

CONTRASTING

Next morning,
Holly, up ahead of me,
walking toward the bus stop.

It's warm for October.

Yell to her,
"Wait up!"

We have time—
suggest we walk to school
through the park
for a change.

    "Sure, I could use the exercise."

I laugh but she just looks at me.

The light's red
but there's no traffic,
           we cross.

I ask her if she's ever heard of
Innovative Arts Academy.

We enter through Mariners' Gates,
"I'm not sure," she says.

I take a picture:
    the tip of an orange leaf in blue sky.

    Contrasting colors in celebration.

POWER DYNAMICS

Holly and I walk by the Seneca Village sign.

> If we went down the hill, made a right,
> we'd find the stream
> where we used to play.

I point out the sign to her
ask when's the last time she read it.
We stop and do.

"It seems pretty silly we used to pretend that the villagers could've
ever stopped the park from being built,"
Holly says.

She's right
      I know she is—
           the nature of urban development plus
           the power dynamics of
           the white population versus
           the African Americans and immigrants
           basically made Central Park inevitable—
but in that sign
I can't help but see

us:

side by side,

stronger together,

holding hands.

STUCK

Fake my way
through first period
Chem.

Next up,
gym.

The teacher makes us do laps.

As I jog,
the rest of the class
          Holly's friends
          Ellery's crush, Taryn
          other kids I don't know
run
     ahead
     ahead
     ahead

their bodies
start to
fly
fly
fly

      up, instead of around

and I lap
lap
lap

on a track by myself.

"Linc, move!
I said running not walking!"

the teacher yells
snaps me out of my vision
             and everyone speeds in front, ahead

until I am circles and circles behind.

BEAM OF LIGHT

After gym, US History.
My teacher,
     Ms. Marshall, strictest in the school,
knows Dad.
          Did an internship with him.
          She was one of the people
          who helped get me into Ketchum.

Today, she says we need to pick a topic
for our sophomore research project.
It will count for 25 percent of our semester grade.

     A 6-week-long study.
     A paper that must include primary source material.

     Found objects, documents, photographs.

My mind   //whirls//   and clicks.

The erasers clap.
The door bursts open.

An idea doesn't just flutter in—
          it   f l i e s.

I don't have to think twice.

After class I run up to her,
name my topic easily.
Ms. Marshall's eyes
light up
when I do.

QUICKENING HEART

That night
Holly
      says her history project topic
         is the suffragettes.

("How interesting!" Mom says.)

I tell her
mine's
Seneca Village.

Holly looks at me,
then down.

("Great choice," says Dad.)

I explain that I'm going to do a photographic essay.

Mom looks at Dad.
Holly defends me,
"She did say we could use photographs."

I give her my most grateful smile.
But then my heart quickens—

      for something this important
      I should take pictures
      on something besides my phone.

I cough.
Deep breaths.
Will she say yes?

DUST OFF

I dare myself.

Ask Mom
if I can use
Uncle Roy's
old Nikon.

"Just for the project.
Please?"

She sighs, goes
into the front hall closet
pulls out the camera from a box.

She wipes off the lens.
Dusts off the strap.
Dabs her eye much too quickly.

"Be careful with it, Linc."

FALLEN CASTLE

There's a photo Mom keeps
on her nightstand
        her brother
        her mother
        herself
                smiling over
                a sand castle.
                Freckly faces, Irish like mine.

Roy died
        a long time ago.
It was an accident, Mom told us.
He fell down stairs,
concussed,
never woke up.

She once told me
he could have been an architect.
Roy would design their castles,
she would help him build.

        She said their summers
        were always the happiest
                at the beach
        //without// her father.

        When I asked why
        she didn't answer,

just kept washing
spotless dishes.

WATCHING

My hand itches for
Roy's Nikon
as I set the table.

During dinner,
utensils clank,
cups clink,
plates empty,
but all I want to do is photograph

the cabinet's edge
the way it cuts into
the ceiling

Mom's shoulders
the way they tense
and rise to meet her ears

Dad's hand
the way it lingers, reaches
for Mom

Holly's smile
the way it shines under
a crown of trophies, awards

my own eyes
the way they capture
the detail of a moment.

Maybe
if I pursued it more seriously—

if I wasn't just good at photography
            but *exceptional*

maybe
my images would have a place
among Holly's trophies, awards.

Maybe
Mom would be able to say
she's proud of her
two successful daughters.

I decide then.

        I will do this.

        I will make her proud.

        Even without their help.

I look down at the groundnut stew,
like it might encourage me.

        Mom never got good
        at doing Holly's hair,
        but she did get good
        at cooking Ghanaian food.

I breathe in
the heavy sauce.

And dream.

THEM/NOT US

I.

When we were ten, we took a family trip to Ghana.
Mom & Dad thought it would be good for all of us
to learn more about where Holly came from.

We learned some Twi phrases,
a common Ghanaian language.
We went to an exhibit
on West African art.

When we went out, the Ghanaian children
would call to all of us, "Oburoni, bra!"
                    ("Foreigner, come!")

It made Holly cry.
Said they weren't supposed
to think of her as a foreigner.
But her American clothes
    her accent
    her holding my hand
gave her away.
                    I cried too—
wanting her
to want
to be like me.

Dad tried to explain to me
how confusing this trip was for Holly.

How as an internationally adopted kid,
she might always also identify
with the country

where she was born.
How that is healthy
but complicated.

I tried my best to understand.

But every time we went somewhere
      a museum
      a market
      a ceremony
I felt sad, knowing
there was a part of Holly
I could never really have.

I felt guilty knowing
      I should
      be happy
that she had us both.

II.

      Toward the end of our trip,
      some Ghanaian women
      taught us how to pound fufuo
         a sticky ball of cassava mixed with plantain.
      Holly took a turn with the huge pestle
      as one woman held the mortar.
      She showed me how
      to add plantain and cassava,
      then we would switch,
      until we formed the fufuo.

After,
      under the dusty red skies
         we ate mangos

juice dripping down our chins
smiling.

Dad told us the Twi version
of *how are you* literally means
how is your body.
And when you say
I am fine you are saying
my body is strong.

Holly and I kept saying the expressions
over & over

"We hon te sɛn?"
"Me hon yɛ!"

Like we were cheering.
We held each other's hands.
Sticky.
Strong.

III.
Before we left,
Mom bought us identical
red-orange dresses.
We wore them
matching
the whole plane ride home.

And even though Holly had Ghana
and I didn't,
I felt better knowing,
no matter what,
I still had Holly.

TWINKLING

Thursday,
Dad gives me money
to get film
for my history project.

Ellery & I go downtown to B&H,
        aisles upon aisles
           of sparkling cameras and film,

I never want to leave—
I still have money left over.

After, we go to a diner.
I listen as Ellery tells me
about Taryn,
the senior girl she's crushed on
for a year.

Ellery listens
as I tell her
the latest
        with Mom and Dad,
      how they want me to focus on
      school and nothing else

        with Holly,
how she was mad I didn't vote
        but is speaking to me again
how even though everything is different now
things feel a bit better than
        they did

with my history project,
how I want to make my mom proud.

She smiles, says she can't wait to see my photos.
        Someday, she knows
they'll all realize how talented I am.

I smile back,
the lights in the
diner twinkle.

HOLD TIGHT

The next night,
home,
                    hold tight to
the extra money from Dad.

With some more instruction,
I could ace this project for history
        use the same pictures
                for my IAA application.
Maybe even ask the photo teacher
to write a recommendation.
Use their
darkroom,
scanners,
printers.

Click through the Westside Center's website   again,
scroll through the classes—
        Intermediate Photography
        would expose me to new techniques,
        match my interests—
until
Holly comes in.

Would she take my side? If she knew?

I close the browser,
click away.

The computer powers itself off.

SOMETHING BIG

Holly's sweaty.
Back from class at Planet Fitness.

"What are you up to?" she asks.
    "Homework," I lie.

She nods her head
    sits at the edge
        of my bed.

Her voice gets   small
    says she wants
    to tell me   "something big."

    Her lips move to the side.
    She cracks her knuckles
    shakes her knee.

Then—
her eyes brighten.
Says she & Stefano plan

to have   //sex//
tomorrow night
        first time.

"You scared?" I ask.
Her mouth opens.
Then   closes.
    Opens again.
"No," she says,
but her eyes say *yes*.

TURN AROUND

Holly & I used to share a room.
A bed.
A blanket even.

We would sleep
            head to feet
share our dreams
as soon as we woke up.

Sometimes, she had nightmares
and I'd wake up to find
      her scarf-wrapped hair
      next to me
her hand on mine.

Now

      I can still tell when she's scared
      but she no longer reaches

                  for my hand.

MESSY

Saturday morning chores.
Mom orders me to clean my room.
Reorganize my desk.

Again.

    "Tidy surfaces make tidy brains."

After Mom leaves,
I text Ellery a photo
of my desk covered
with papers and books
and write
drowning.

She writes me back,
same here.
And then sends me a smiley tree
with a slogan
that says, "I beleaf in you."

I text her a best friend heart, then
I order and sort.

Mom approved Holly's room an hour ago,
but I wonder
if she would approve
of what her precious daughter
is about to do.
A pigeon appears outside my window
bobbing his head
in answer.

GHOSTS #1

Once my room is finished,
    with my new film
        my old Nikon
        my Seneca Village map
I head to the park.

On the map, I see:
Near where there once was a church,
there is now a playground.

I spot one girl with chalk
drawing swirls on the pavement.

I take pictures
of kids   running
        laughing
        crying
        crawling
over ground that once held the prayers
of a community.

Years ago
on this same playground,
Holly pushed the tire swing
as I held firm to the rope.

We didn't need anyone else.

She jumped up onto the swing.
We sat across from each other
until we took flight
and even the sun followed.

WHOLENESS

When I get home
Holly's doing yoga.
I hear the recording going.

>   *Inhale up,*
>   *exhale down.*

I imagine the photos I just took
        in my mind's eye:
The composition of the old boulder
        peering into the playground.
The way the light
        hits the swings.
The contrast in the kids crying
        with the ones laughing.

I know
there is potential.

~~Take a few deep breaths myself,
try to hold still,
but I can't bury this feeling.~~
Don't want to.

The application is due 11/15,
only five weeks away.
Only five weeks to build a portfolio.

I look at the brochure
from the Westside Center
        the Intermediate Photo class,

the class that starts next week,
the class that costs more than I have saved.

I don't know
      yet
how to pay the whole
$350

but
I do know this:
This is something I have to do.

I fill out the registration form.

Inhale up,
exhale down.

SATURDAY NIGHT

Holly has her "going out" music on,
        as much a part of her routine
        as homework,
        soccer practice,
        yoga.

Mom at work, on-call,
Dad and I have a plan
to watch our show.
Mostly we watch fantasies.

Before Holly leaves
        hair perfectly straightened
        best jeans
        makeup just right—

                hard not to wonder
                if she will look different
                     after.
I ask if she wants to talk about   it.

She says no but thanks.
Says she's excited.
Squeezes my hand.

After she leaves,
I rub the spot
where her hand gripped mine.

Whisper, "Good luck?"
to the space
she left behind.

HAZY LIGHT

Before our show starts
I go out
    get Dad & me ice cream.

But the way the lights flicker
above the park
calls to me.
The night set aglow.

I

enter.

Promise myself I'll be quick.

Follow the hazy light
down paths
past people
but I'm stopped
      drawn
by the carousel,
horses still
    silent
in the night.

I walk closer.

There's a guy there
with blue hair—
smoking an electronic cigarette.

In the dark, the light from it
        a firefly.

I take a picture of this boy—

                his light—

                all those colored horses
                inside a ring

                        and huge trees

            limbs like arms
                    hovering.

Watching and clicking
my insides spark alive
color gleaming
in the blanketed darkness.

                            Floating,

then
force myself to
rejoin the world
            beyond the park.

BORN TO BE

When I get home,
Dad asks what took so long.

"I couldn't decide
which flavors to get."

He chuckles,
seems to believe me.

We each grab a spoon, dig in.

At the very same time, we say yum.

Before I can stop it,
thoughts creep in:

> What would it have been like
> if it had been just us?
>
> What would it have been like
> never knowing
> I had a better-than-me sister
>   with a fuller-than-mine life?
>
> What would it have been like
> never facing
> disappointment
> from a never-happy-with-me mother?

If it had been just us,
maybe Dad would've let me be
just who I was born to be.

INVASION

In the middle of our show,
       the elves invading the gnomes,
a text from Ellery:

WE HOOKED UP!
Emojis parade behind the words.

Of course I know she means
Taryn.

What do you say to that?

I write: **OMG Congrats**
but as I do
my heart sags.

Holly & Stefano,
now Ellery & Taryn.

still //just//

click//
click//
Linc.

ALMOST

I strain to hear the door
when Holly comes home.

      Hear the water running
      as she brushes her teeth,
      washes her face.

I head next door
to ask her how it was.

But when I do,
      I hear her on the phone
      giggling.
Maggs.

I turn
          around
go back to my room.

I sketch on my wall.
      Two tiny birds
         walking
         in a line
              on
              a
              tightrope.

Take a picture of it for Ellery
and send.

I keep checking my phone until I fall asleep
but she never writes back.

RESTS

Sunday,
I wake up to
a flurry of texts from Ellery.
How amazing Taryn is.
How smart.
Hot.
But not one caption
for the image I sent.

Before breakfast,
Holly comes to me,
says:
"It was perfect."

A part of me
wants to believe her.

But her eyes give it away,
she blinks too many times.

Her smile stays wide, though.

I give a small smile back.

Holly forgave me for not voting,
she helped me get Roy's camera,
maybe I owe it to her
to believe her?

"I'm happy for you, Holly."
I try to sound like
I mean it.

OUR SUNDAY RELIGION

I.

By Sunday afternoon,
Holly has somehow
lost her virginity
but also done her homework
                    chores
                    gone for a run.

She spins in a swirl of gold stars.

She helps Mom & Dad
finish the Sunday crossword puzzle,
        building bridges made
of esoteric words.

While I count my money,
try to figure out how to pay
for the photo class at the Center,
Mom enters.

        No knock.

        Wineglass in hand.

I knew she was coming.

Weekdays she spot-checks,
Sundays she reads through
every
single
assignment.

This is our religion:

Devotions began in sixth grade,
when my
"overactive imagination"
became laziness, procrastination.

        Sidestepping the truth:
I'm just not—
won't ever be—
book smart.

Leave Mom with the start
of my lab report,
a short English essay,
a set of math problems,
tell her I'm going outside
to work on my history project.

Run for the park,
camera swinging.

II.
There
      I focus
on a path in the center
of where Seneca Village once stood.
Two little girls,

      skipping,
      holding hands.

There
      I see

the rock outcropping
that sits across from where
the All Angels (integrated) Church
once stood.

As I snap photos of
the black-and-white stone
I command the colors to blur.

Envision myself with
   a teacher
   a class
   a way
to capture this history better.

III.

Home two hours later.
Mom greets me,
pacing,
her mouth a tight line,
drink in hand,
she guides me into my room.
"To talk."

Worse than weeknights,
Sundays are when her voice
gets louder,
meaner.

     Sunday is the day she drinks.

     When we were younger, she never did.
     But now—libations have been added
     to our Sunday tradition—

the only day when she says
everything she thinks.

She pulls lines from her "Bible":

"How can you still not understand this stuff?"

"What's wrong with you?"

"When will you take your work seriously?"

Every assignment lined with red.

I bend my head,
        another ritual,
whisper sorry.

She tells me that's not enough.
Makes me sit down at my desk.
Watches me
as I make
each correction.

My hand shakes.
Problems blur
and then when she yells
"Focus, Linc, Jesus"—

I do, I do.

I try, I try.
Finally,
she leaves to pour another glass.
                    Then another.

A few more than usual.

She's done with me.

I hear her bedroom door close.

And the whole house sighs in relief.

Amen.

EXCUSES

Dad comes in
like he does every time this happens,

    delivers snacks, sympathies,
    makes excuses for Mom:
        She just wants what's best for you.
        She's been stressed at work.

Holly comes in
like she does every time this happens,

    tries to distract me with some gossip
    about kids I hardly know:
        Cara got dumped by Seth,
        Liam finally came out.

But there's something else
I want to talk about.

"Did you notice Mom drank more
than usual today?"

Holly flicks her wrist.
Cracks her neck.

She says yes
then continues on
about Cara and Seth.

After she leaves,
I stay in my room

like I do every time this happens,

    work on the details
    in my wall sketches:
        shading petals,
        growing stems.

Then take pictures of each drawing,
intensify their color.
Dim.
Intensify.

ALLOWANCES

Monday,
Mom
leaves our allowances
on the table
plus

a note for Holly:
Have a great day!

One for me:
Attitude is everything. Make today count!

As if I can change
the inferior functioning
of my own brain
just by thinking positively.

I grab my bag
  stash the money
  throw the note

in the trash.

Imagine it
bursting into flames.

CIRCLES

At lunch, Taryn sits with us.
> Both sides of her head shaved,
> the hair on top flops to the side.
> A Jewish star around her neck.

> > She tosses me a *hey*.
> > I throw a *hey* back.
> > Taryn doesn't say anything else
> > to me, her eyes stuck on Ellery.

Ellery asks about my weekend.
I tell her it was like every other weekend.
She blushes, says
> ~~more to Taryn than to me~~
hers wasn't.
As if that wasn't obvious already.

> She & Taryn
> draw a circle
> around themselves,
> me on the periphery.
> They sit shoulder to shoulder
> curl in together just like
> > Holly & Stefano

> so close
> they push everyone else
> farther out.
If I ever find someone
> of my own
> > we won't be a circle
but something with edges
and openings.

INSTINCT

After lunch, in the hallway—
I'm behind
Stefano
and his friends

when I hear him say

"she finally gave it up."

Watch him high-five,
receive congrats.

It was perfect,
she said.

My body goes stiff.

It's not a choice
I make
so much as a
reflex—

I shove him
as hard as I can.

PREDATORS

He's caught off guard
       stumbles forward
       turns around.

Sees it's me.

"What the hell, Linc?"

His friends surround him,
laugh.

I am small
in comparison
but I
feel

huge.

Ellery bounds up to my side.

       Right to his face I say:

"Don't ever talk about Holly that way."

A crowd gathers

       Stefano and I   eyes deadlocked

           neither one of us prey

when the vice principal
sprouts from the center.

WEIGHT

We're taken to the office.

Stefano is seen first.

Ellery waits with me,
keeps asking me what Stefano said
to make me so upset.

I don't tell her Holly's business,
shrug off her questions.

Mr. Chapman calls me in,
Ellery says, "Good luck."

He asks what happened.

What happened is that
Stefano is an asshole.
He doesn't deserve my sister.

    If my words held weight,
    he wouldn't be
    the other half   of her circle.

SUSPENDED

The vice principal says
academic probation
plus this "act of violence"

equals
        suspension
        for a week.

Mr. Chapman looks at me
sympathetically, leaves.

My parents are called,
one of them has to take me home

even though I usually
go back and forth to school
all the time

//alone.//

        My stomach spins—
                        Mom.
        Her anger.
        Her disappointment.

        Suddenly,
        my mind catches up—

        what does this mean for my permanent record?
        My GPA?
        (and IAA?)

I watch the vice principal on the phone,
focus on its cord,
how she curls it around her finger.

She doesn't reach my mom.
Tries again.
        Dad.

Exhale.
At least he can
break the news to her.

        "Unfortunately, Mr. Malone, Linc's been suspended."

I watch her skywrite the words
I watch them hang in the air

            then slowly disappear.

STUCK

On the bus home,
        stuck in crosstown traffic,
Dad asks me
        to explain.

How do I explain without
betraying Holly?

"I just don't like him"
is all I can think to say.

        "That doesn't mean it's okay
        to shove him."

A woman on the bus gives us a sideways glance.
The bus wheezes all the way to a halt.

        Then:
        "You know what we historians say?"

I say back to him,
        not for the first time in my life,
"Humans are their choices."

And as I do,

everything red turns green

a breeze flies through the bus

traffic starts moving.

CUT & PASTE

When I get home
Dad goes right to his desk.

Humans are their choices.

I go to my room
count my cash again
          $40 left over from B&H,
          $200 now saved from allowance
                    $110 to go.

I know everything
would be different
if I could take a photo class
          go to school
somewhere
else,
somewhere
I fit in,
somewhere
that takes the arts
          takes *me*
seriously.

My choice is clear.

          Cut out: failure, disappointment, suspension.
          Paste in: success, pride, creation.

CONSIDERATIONS

My phone pings.
A text from Ellery.

You ok? What happened?

I tell her I'm in deep shit.

She says she's sorry,
tells me to hang in there.

I have too much to do
to write back.

Before Mom gets home
        angry
I send her & Dad an email:

I'm sorry. I know I messed up today.
I know you worked hard to get me into that school.
But would you consider letting me go here, instead?
I will do everything I need to do to get in.
Remember the brochure I showed you?
There's even a photography class nearby where I could
learn a lot of techniques so I would have the skills I need
to apply.
www.innovativeartsacademyofnyc.edu

Love,
Linc

STONE CASTLE

Holly swings open the door,
I jump.

      "How dare you do this to him—to me?"

She stands above me,
defends her evil prince,
the stone castle they've built.

"He said something awful."
Her face flashes fear.
      "What?"

"That you had finally given it up.
He was telling other guys. I had to—"

She shuts her eyes tight.
Her lips move side to side.
She opens her eyes, says:

      "Whatever, Linc. You're just jealous.
      I see how you look at him.
      I know you've never liked him."

She slams down my schoolwork,
everything of mine
she had to carry home.

Then—
shuts the door
in my face.

CONTINUOUS FOCUS

On a digital camera,
you can press
continuous focus,
keep an image
clear
even as it moves.

In my head,
       all through a somber dinner of leftovers,
           microwave beeping
           silverware scraping
           hardly any talking,
I keep continuous focus
on IAA.

Afterward
Mom & Dad
come into my room.

At first
no one speaks.

Then finally,

       "Linc, we looked at that website.
       I'm sorry, but we will not reward you
       for jeopardizing your future,"
       says Dad.

"But this is *about* my future!"
I say.

"We cannot support your desire
    to go to art school. And what makes you think
    you can even handle extracurriculars?
    The only thing you should be focused on
    is your schoolwork!"

says Mom.
They take my phone.
        "You're grounded."

My eyes blur
but my mind holds on
        with continuous focus
sharp,
locked
on what I want.

STAINS

In the morning,
Dad wakes me up
as if I were going to school.
Even though I'm suspended
I still have to do homework,
he says.

In bigger trouble than usual,
but not even Holly
comes to talk to me
this time.

Instead she yells at me
to get out of the bathroom.

Sweeps past me
without a word
when I open the door.

A few minutes later,
I hear her and Mom joking
in the kitchen,
making smoothies
      kale banana strawberry
            their favorite.

I pull my camera out.
Try to capture this feeling.

I take pictures

fingerprints on the window,
hair shadowing the blanket,
a layer of dust,

until they're all my eye can see.

They don't care
about my dreams,
so I do what I have to—
dare myself—
sneak to the petty cash drawer,
the one Mom and Dad keep
for food delivery, quick errands.

20, 40, 60, 80
plenty there—
I take what I need.

CERTAINTY

Dad says he's working
from home
to monitor
my suspension.

What do they think I'm going to do?

I start with chemistry.
Dad helps me
balance equations
//the right way.//

As I do,
my mind flashes—
to Holly, who loves
the certainty of
     math
     science
     questions that have only
         one correct answer.

Questions like

Didn't I have the right to defend my sister?
Don't families stick together?

BLANK LEAVES

I.

In second grade,
we had to make family trees.

Holly left most of her leaves

blank.

When she brought it home,
I filled her leaves in
with all of our relatives.

I thought
she forgot
their names.
I thought
she needed my help.

When she saw what I'd done
she screamed
cried
hid my favorite toy
but wouldn't tell me
why.

Mom told me I shouldn't write on my sister's work.
Dad told me he knew I didn't mean to do anything wrong.

But—

that night she slept with Mom & Dad,

I cried into my pillow, slept alone.

II.
The next day

Holly hugged me and handed me a Twix bar

left over from Halloween.

"One for one?"
she asked.

A peace offering.

"One for one,"

I said,

handing her a Twizzlers,
her favorite.

And we never said anything more.

III.
Later,
Dad explained
Holly was upset
because she wanted
the teacher to know
she was adopted.

He told me
he knew I was

just trying to help,
but next time,
I shouldn't interfere with what belongs to her.

There are so many angles

to right
to wrong.

TRANSFORMING

I grab the money,
my registration form.

> No more interfering with Holly's life.
> Time to make something of my own.

I tell Dad I need to work on
my history project.

> "Can I go to the park?"

He looks over my other homework
then says, "I'll come with you."

I look down.

> Grass withers under my feet.

SWIRLING

We walk together
     through the bright autumn sun
     red oak leaves swirl around our feet
glide past
       joggers, strollers,
to where Seneca Village used to be.

Make the most of it for now,
take notes as
Dad tells me how
the idea for Central Park
came from an anonymous source.

     A gentleman who,
     after visiting the elegant European cities,
     decided New York
     needed a large park too.

He wrote about it in the newspaper.
Said it was what the city
was missing.

Dad continues, says,
"Originally the park
was going to be along the East River."

     "What happened?"
     I ask.

"The owners of that land wouldn't sell."

I think of the people who lived here

            poor
            immigrants
who couldn't defend their land
from wealthy buyers.

            "The park's pretty.
            But that seems unfair."

Dad puts his arm around me then,
as we walk,
and says,

"You know I don't approve
of violence.

Period.

But—my missing Linc—
it's nice being with you
here,
today."

Dad's arm
around me feels light

but the guilt
lands heavy.

OVERLAPPING SHADOWS

Sitting on a bench,
we look at my maps
together.

     My stomach sinks
     with the weight of
          stolen money
          class registration form
     in my pocket.

But click/click/
with continuous focus
I look back down at the map.

I tell Dad I want to take pictures
of the places now
that were a part of the village
then—
     a before and after
     of one of New York's iconic spaces.

"What are you hoping to say
through those photos?"
he asks.

I stop
realize:
I don't know.

Dad tells me to
stick with it,
I will figure it out.

He asks if I am ready to go.
I ask for a little more time.

To "consider my project's direction."
He grins, says he trusts me
to be home in an hour.
Tells me this is a risk
he hopes he will not regret.

Shame takes his place beside me
as he leaves me in the park.

The shadows of a couple
pass by.

They overlap with
a stranger's beside them.
But none of them notice.

Just before leaving,
I take a photo,
capture the place
they overlap.

People's shadows
floating through
the paths of a history
they never knew.

COLOR ADJUSTMENT

I make sure I still have
at least twenty minutes,
walk
to the Westside Center.

The same receptionist
        smiling sweetly behind the counter
takes my bundle of money,
        my registration form.

Says the class starts this Saturday,
        October 20th, runs 8 weeks.

                        Despite my suspension
                        despite the stealing

I'm sure
        in his heart
Dad would want this for me.

The trees outside light up
in confirmation.

I feel **powerful**
        like where I'm heading
        is **brighter** than where I've been.

Like when you realize
your photo could be just how you imagined it

                if you simply adjust the colors.
                And so you do.

DEPTH OF FIELD

On return,
I shout hello to
Dad in his office.

I swell with warmth
like I've swallowed
the sun.

In my field of vision,

a framed picture
of Roy on the mantel.

I walk closer.

He's looking up from a book, smiling.

Last year in Photo 1, we learned
there's a shallow depth of field
in portraits—

Roy's face is in focus but
what's around him is soft, blurred,
not like a landscape
where everything is sharp.

How much longer after this photo was taken did he die?

I touch the floaty space around him,
tell him I'm going to find my future,
and thank him for his camera.
Watch him smile in reply.

IN FRONT/BEHIND

My eyes drift then
to our sixth grade school pictures.

    Holly
    beaming bright.

    Me
    fake smiling.

Not sure what anyone thought
when they looked at me.
Never as smart or pretty as Holly.
Never comfortable under
    the watchful eyes of others.

Now
I'm the one
behind the lens
    a place of power,
        creation.

Before I leave the mantel

I

blow a kiss to Roy,
turn my photo
upside down.

SCHEDULING

Wednesday, in between homework,
                    studying for my chemistry test,
                    practicing with Roy's camera,
I make a schedule
to keep myself on track.
Mom would be proud,
if she knew.
If I could share it with her.

10/20: Photo Class 1
10/27: Photo Class 2
11/3: Photo Class 3
11/5: ROUGH DRAFT due for HISTORY PROJECT
(use same photos for project & IAA app)
11/10: Photo Class 4
11/15: IAA DEADLINE, application postmark date!
    Checklist: 12 portfolio pieces, Artist's Statement, applica-
    tion, teacher recommendation (from Westside teacher?)
11/17: Photo Class 5
11/19: FINAL HISTORY PROJECT DUE
11/24: No class Thanksgiving Weekend
12/1: Photo Class 6
12/8: Photo Class 7
12/15: Photo Class 8
Jan?: Hear back from IAA
Sept: Go to IAA for junior year!!

I can't tack it up in my room
so I fold it neatly
    place it in my desk drawer
    frame it in my mind.

SURREALISM

Thursday,
> Holly delivers me homework
> but she hardly speaks to me.

Friday,
> Ellery emails
> > asks how I am.
> Says she hates not being able
> > to text me,
> > she's missed me all week.

Saturday,
> my heart quickens
> *I'm going to make something of my own.*
>
> I put on my best jeans,
> my T-shirt of the Magritte painting,
> the one with the apple.
>
> Tell my parents I'm going to work in the park.
> Dad & Mom look at each other.
> Dad tells Mom I'm really working hard.
> Holly looks up
> > mid-stretch
> then back down,
> > just as quick.
>
> I pretend
> I don't care that
> she's ignoring me.

Click/click/past
Click/click/present

Dad says,
"Here, take this,"
hands me back my phone.
Says I should have it
if I am going to be out
alone.

Mom shakes her head,
like I don't deserve it.

Mom,
in her Mean Queen voice,
"Don't make us regret this, Linc."

Grab Roy's camera,
my map,
pretend to walk to the park.

Then—

        a taxi honks
        the camera flashes
        a pigeon turns around.

When no one's looking
I turn the other way
quick
and

click/click
run.

LIGHT-HEADED
PHOTO CLASS #1, SATURDAY, OCTOBER 20TH
26 DAYS UNTIL IAA APPLICATION DUE

I arrive at the Center,
  scan the room,
   hope I don't see anyone I know:
     A man
         maybe seventy.
     Two
         middle-aged women.
     Some
         other teens.
But then—

someone who looks my age
someone I recognize—

the blue-haired guy
from the carousel.

Eyes focused on his camera
     looking critically at the image on-screen.

His hair so blue,
I taste Popsicles, bubble gum.

Slide in next to him.

   He looks up.

      When I look into his eyes,
      he holds my gaze.

Strong cheekbones.
Olive skin.
Pink lips.
His faded gray T-shirt reads:
"I'm Going to Be a Grandpa."
I congratulate him
on the soon-to-be birth
of his grandson.

He laughs, says his name's Silas.

Tell him mine,
ask him what his children
are naming their kid.

"Vern," he says, no hesitation.

STRENGTHENING

I'm still laughing
when
the teacher,
        Fiona,
starts class.

        She pushes up her glasses over tight curls, says,
        "Welcome to Intermediate Photography.
        We'll be together three hours
        every Saturday
        for the next several weeks."

        She points to drawers we can label with our names,
        a place to store our prints.

        She says
        because we all have
        some fundamental understanding of photography
        we can take photographs
        of anything we choose for this class.

        But we will critique each other's work
        and she will show us how to make our own
        stronger.
        Different techniques we can use.

        "This is an exciting time to be a photographer.
        There's so much we can do with color.
        We can be painters too."

Then she asks us to tell a little bit about ourselves:
who we are

126

and
why we're here.

Silas says the reason he's here
is that he feels most alive
when he's capturing images.

                    A tingling passes through me.

When it's my turn
I tell them the truth:

I want to go to art school,
I need to learn more.
This is what I want to do with my life.

As we go around my fingers burn,

there's an energy in this place
                    these people
I wish I could capture
                    color
                    keep.

MIND-CAMERAS

Fiona says
to be a real photographer
your mind-camera—

> the part of your brain that pictures
> the way an image will turn out

> the part of your brain that pictures
> what isn't there
> but could be—

must be on high alert,

tuning in
> to your surroundings
at all times.

I think of my own mind-camera
how sometimes it feels
like it's on overdrive

how I can hardly
ever

turn it off.

Maybe, here, finally—
my mind-camera will be worth something—

not a curse
not a distraction
but a gift.

COMPOSITION

Fiona projects on-screen:

> a bird's wing
> > half a face   a blurry bluish space.

Asks us to use our "mind-cameras,"
share what the images convey.

> Silas, not shy, calls out:
> "Flying—"

Then he looks at me.
I look back, away.

An older man:
> "Dreaming—"

> "Loneliness,"
> I say.

"What about now?"
She shows

> the whole bird.
> The whole face.
> The blue, a sliver of sky.

"Freedom!"
> "Harmony!"
> > "Reflection!"

"You see? Composition changes everything," she says.

Just an hour ago,
I was with my family,
together but alone.
Now, looking around me,
I know
I have more in common
with these other artists
than anyone at home.

TRACING

After class,
Silas,
        so tall he towers over me,
asks what I'm up to.
I tell him I have to be home
in thirty minutes
but first
I'm going to the park
to take some pictures.
He says, "Cool, mind if I come?"

My heart's shutter speeds up.

But when we get there,
he takes off for the Meadow.
Says he'll circle back.

I watch him till he vanishes,
then focus in on:
        short person/ tall
        pale person/ brown
        young person/ old.

All these people who exist
        right now
never even knowing
they trace footsteps
from another time and space.

How can I frame them
like ghosts of a past
they never knew?

COMMUTING

Fifteen minutes later
Silas returns.
Ten minutes until
I need to be home.

"I got shots of mimes
performing in 'an orchestra,'"
he says.

I tell him that sounds epic.

Ask him how he heard about the Center.

Says his parents are divorced,
Mom, downtown, Dad, up.
His dad suggested the Center,
something "positive" for him to do on the weekends
so he wasn't always going back
downtown to see his friends.

His stepsister is usually there anyway,
she and his dad fight a lot.
Good to get out of the house.

He asks how long
I've been into photography.

I tell him about Photo 1,
how I take pictures with my phone.
Now with my uncle's old camera too.
Tell him about my history project.
He seems to really listen.

It starts to drizzle.

"I should go,"
I say.
He gets up with me.

Our footsteps
fall
in line.

As we walk
Silas asks
what's a name like Linc, anyway.

"My dad named me.
I was a surprise pregnancy.
            Their missing link."

        Look at the time.
Shit.
I'm five minutes late.

The rain falls faster,
I speed up toward home,
tell him I don't want to go
but I can't get in any more trouble.

He laughs, says he knows how that goes.
Touches my hand,
asks if we can get together
again
sometime—
        outside of class.

Everything feels like it's happening
at lightning speed,
but somehow I'm not scared.

I practically yell, "Yes!"

He nods,
"Cool,"

pulls out his electronic cigarette
then disappears down the block.

I reach the steps of our brownstone
look at the bird
carved into the side.

Its eyes blink twice at me,
    wings flutter,
        then fly.

DEVELOPING

AUTOMATIC FLASH

In the door, ten minutes late.
Mom gives me a look.
Dad asks me how it went.
"Great!" I say, heart pounding.
Silas asked me out?!
A raindrop drips down
my cheek,
I open my mouth
catch it.
For a minute
(flash)
I wish Holly
and I were speaking.
Wish I
could tell her my news.
Text Ellery instead.
She sends a parade of happy dancers.
Then she says: Tell me everything Monday.
Ellery would like Silas.
They're both artists.
And so
//flash//
am I.

ARTIST'S STATEMENT FOR INNOVATIVE ARTS ACADEMY APPLICATION

Artists express the world the way they see it. Oftentimes, they see things in unusual ways—sometimes they even see what isn't actually there but could be. My vision as a photographer is to show that there is more than one layer of truth to any given moment. One example of this is how the past lives on in the present.

I have always felt better at expressing myself, more understood, through images. At a school like IAA, I believe I would be surrounded by others who could relate to this experience.

MY OWN SETTLEMENT

I start off strong, then
blank
blank
blank.

What else can I say about my vision?
What truth am I trying to capture?

I wander into the den,
try to get un-
stuck.

Dad, Mom & Holly are playing
one of their games.
My parents say hi,
Holly does not.

They:
Like German strategy games,
   Carcassone, Agricola, Settlers of Catan.
A trio
hunched around boards,
capturing places
like I do photos.

I:
Used to try to play,
always got distracted, bored.

Then:
Mom would tell me to
focus, pay attention.

Now:
No one invites me to play.
I move back to my room.

> *What is your vision?*
> *What truth are you trying to capture with your art?*

No words come.
I draw on the corner behind my bed.

Settle:
My own community.

> Blue-haired mermaids bathing on rocks.
> A huge blue sun,
> pink and orange clouds
> stretched across the sky like wings.

TRACES

Sunday,
Mom's wineglass out,
Dad saves me
      accompanies me again
to the park.

I ask him if he's noticed
Mom drinking more lately.

He says she's just been
a bit stressed. Not to worry.

Changes the subject
back to the park.

    Tells me about the day
    the villagers had to leave.

    October 1st, 1857.

    African American citizens of Seneca Village
    and "Pigtown,"
        a neighborhood of Irish immigrants just south,
    Germans scattered throughout,
    all 1,600 people
    forced to leave their homes.

    Barely left traces of their
        schools
        churches
        farms.

There was an excavation, Dad says,
some years back:
They would dig and refill
the site in the park overnight.
They found:
> a child's shoe
> a roasting pan
> a teakettle
> an entire foundation wall
>> of the All Angels' sexton's home.

While he talks, I take photographs of
where the churches were,
> the school.

Focus in on people
with clasped hands,
reading books,
in those very same spots—

merging present with past.

REWORK

When I get home,
Mom is in her room,
she's already checked
all my homework.

She says the answers
are mostly right
but my work is sloppy.
I need to proofread,
          show all my work.

I take a chance,
dart to my room.

How can I make myself better at this?
Bring up my GPA?

          I need to do better in
          science and math
          history and gym
          for a 2.7 overall.

In the darkroom,
last year in Photo 1,
          the teacher switched
          developing prints
          from bath to bath,
          said—

          "Chemistry
          is as essential to photography
          as creativity."

So I force myself to try harder.

Show all the steps to the problem.
Try to see science
as something essential.

Necessary to my craft.
Mom peeks in as I do.
I feel her stare,
  press down so hard
on the pencil
it breaks in two.

TUNE OUT

Monday again—
suspension over.

Overnight,
Silas texted me
  hey what's up.
My heart races.

I trail
  steps behind
Maggs & Holly
on the way to school.

Their matching calf muscles
  in stride, so strong
    the concrete retracts for them.

Earbuds in,
tune them out,

  notice
  where the still-green grass pokes through
  the concrete

   in quiet rebellion.

Take a picture.
Send it to Silas.
    Turn up the song,
    turn down a new corner.
I stop following them
    take a route all my own.

DANGLING

I swerve & turn
all the way to school.

No response
from Silas yet.

> In the hall,
> Stefano
>   calls out to Ethan
> who shouts to Maggs
>   who tags Holly
>   who's still ignoring me

>   and all their friends surround.

I am careful
to avoid them
            {
they are the ~web~
            }
and me,
a

     spider

no thread.

ABOUT (WITHOUT) ME

After lunch,
Ellery walks me to
my weekly meeting
with Mr. Chapman.
Assures me Silas will write back.

When I open the door,
both my parents are there.
And the principal.
I freeze.

The ceiling fan
      spins   on
a cabinet
     opens   closes.

    What the hell?

Dad's hand rests on Mom's knee.
The principal rubs one temple.

    "Linc, please, sit."

Legs shake as I do.

    "Your parents and I have been talking.
    We are disappointed in your behavior.
    But they assure me this violent outburst was atypical.
    They assure me you will behave.
    Mr. Chapman says you have been following through
    with your weekly meetings and handing in your work
    with success."

My cheeks burn.

"We will give you one final opportunity."

Mom nods
    thanks him effusively
    glares at me
so

I murmur some promises,
            apologies.

Though for this meeting
     about me
it seems like

         I'm their paper doll
            a cutout
          that they make walk and talk
           the way they want

I didn't need to be here at all.

DISTORTIONS

"One final chance.
This is it,"
Mom says,
like I haven't already heard.

Roll my eyes.
                    "I get it."

The hallways press in around us,
like we're in a house of mirrors.

            Our limbs **stretch**, then shrink

f r a g m e n t e d, distorted.

"Listen to me, Linc.
You will work harder than you've ever worked.
Is that clear?"

            I smile to myself.
            She doesn't know about
            the GPA preference for IAA.

So when I promise her I will,
my image ~~*wobbles*~~

then

stills.

It's not a lie.

HAND ON WINDOW

Silas texts back after school: **great shot.**
My heart leaps.

All week
we send each other filtered images:
streetlights,
windows,
shadows.

We change what's dark
to light.
Light to dark.

All week
I focus
on schoolwork, IAA.

> For each set of problems I work on,
> each reading I finish,

I spend time on my application.

> Reread the Artist's Statement details.

> > *What is your vision?*
> > *What truth are you trying to capture with your
> > art?*

The questions bark at me.

> I take a photo
> of my hand

between the windowpane
and the security bars.

Light leaks around each finger.
Light that seeps in.
Light that demands to be seen.
Even if I try to block it.

How much am I capturing something with my art

as much as I am   releasing it?

ARTIST'S STATEMENT FOR INNOVATIVE ARTS ACADEMY APPLICATION

Artists express the world the way they see it. Oftentimes, they see things in unusual ways—sometimes they even see what isn't actually there but could be. My vision as a photographer is to show that there is more than one truth to any given moment. One example of this is how the past lives on in the present.

I have always felt better at expressing myself, more understood, through images. At a school like IAA, I believe I would be surrounded by others who could relate to this experience. **Whether someone is sculpting, painting, acting, dancing, singing or taking a photograph, they are offering something to an audience. They are offering art and creativity. And through that art, the viewer is exposed to a new perspective.**

I come from a family who sees academic achievement as the height of success. Maybe at IAA my viewpoint will be seen as valid, essential, necessary.

SHOCKWAVE

I work harder
than I've ever worked before,
just like I promised I would.

Thursday night,
      Dad tells me
      he's noticed
      and he's proud.

      Mom nods in agreement,
      says she's impressed
      with my focus,
            says I'm no longer
            grounded.

I stop, mid-chew.

Even Holly looks up in surprise.

      The chandelier blinks twice.
      The curtains fly up and down.
      Our chairs spin.

Mom says
      that I'm walking
      a fine line,
but today

      the floor trembles

I'm on the right side of it.

A tidal wave of guilt threatens
to unleash
      the stolen money
      the photo class
      the IAA application

but Mom is so busy smiling at me
that despite the storm inside
      despite silence still from Holly

I let myself smile right back.

UNEARTHED

After school on Friday,
Ellery asks if I want to hang
with her and Taryn and Taryn's friends,
but I tell her I need to work.

I focus on my history project
read my notes from online sources:

> "Seneca Village brought stability and community
> to the persecuted . . ."
>> in 1853 ground was broken
>> to erect the AME Zion Church,
> "but it was a brief reprieve . . .
> wealthy buyers destroyed everything."
>> Just a few years later
>> it was demolished
>> along with the African Union Church,
>> Colored School #3.

I take pictures of
    bikers
    runners
    Rollerbladers

                      as they whiz past

a history so deep
no one ever stops running
to see.

I take photos
to try to show I do.

SPIN & CHANGE

That night:

> Can you hang out?
>> Silas asks.
> Bored & at my dad's.

Mom & Dad at a work function.
Holly is sleeping at Maggs's.

I'm not grounded anymore, right?
Either way, no one will know that I'm

                              gone.

I text him back

Meet me in the park?

and as I do,
the streetlight
outside my window

                    spins
                    changes colors

transforms into a disco ball.

FOUNDATION

We meet at Mariners' Gates.
He tells me I look good.

I blush and
ask him about his week.
      He says same old shit—
      school, parents on his case.

I tell him I want to show him
something cool about the park.
Guide him to the spot.

As we stand
      on top
      of the square of cobblestones
      in the ground
      on the hill
      of the park,
      I say:
            "Did you know
            historians used to think these stones
            were remnants
            of the original All Angels' Church
            foundation?

            When they excavated,
            they realized their mistake—
            a theory surfaced—
            the stones just remnants
            of a hot dog stand from the '50s.
            Most of the church
            was actually moved,

        beam by beam,
        to a new location."

Silas nods but doesn't speak.

I realize
I sound like Dad.
Suddenly
I'm self-conscious.

The silence is awkward
but trees envelop us,
his brown eyes dive into me.

"That's one cool fact,"
he says.

"Well, it's really just a theory—"

He puts his finger over my lips.

        Then his arms around my hips.
                I reach down,
pull them up,
            our fingers entwine like branches.

As he leans down,   I lean into him.
        My first kiss.

        On top of these stones
        we form our own
        foundation.

SWIRLING

After,
Silas walks me to the corner.

        The wind picks   up.

He kisses me one more time
asks if we can see each other
tomorrow, after class.

        I tell him   yes.

He smiles
      hands lingering on my waist
then heads home the other way.
I watch him go
and, as I do,
press my hand to my lips.
Holding on to
my very first kiss.

My mind-camera clicks on
and I am flipping through
a photo album
      on the cover
      engraved letters swirl
      into each other

      Silas & Linc   *Linc & Silas*

LEADING

As I walk up to the house,
Holly stands in the doorway
        with her key.
The light from the entry
shines on us.

She asks:
        "Where were you?"
just as I say:
        "Why are you home?"

We break into
simultaneous smiles.

Then she says
she & Maggs had a fight
didn't wanna stay there.

My heart jumps.
Holly's actually speaking to me?

I consider telling
her about Silas.

But instead
I open the door for her,
let the light lead us in.

CHANGING THE SUBJECT

She says they were out to dinner
on a double date.

> "I don't know how we got on the subject but—

> everyone started asking me about
> what it's like to be adopted.
> To have parents who are a different race—

> Stefano and Ethan had some interesting questions—"

Holly pauses.
The name Stefano
drives a wall between us.

"They had interesting questions . . . ?"
I try to knock the wall down.

> "Yeah. Like how being in a white family changed
> my experience, if I had ever felt discriminated against—
> if I felt like I experienced it more or less—"

"What did you say?"

Holly waves her hand.
Like I asked the wrong question.

> "Maggs kept shutting me up.
> Changing the subject.

> Then she made me go with her
> to the bathroom,

said it wasn't sexy to talk about discrimination.
I told her they were the ones asking me—
but she said I should've just changed the subject."

Holly moves her lips to the side.
Shakes her head.

"But Maggs is mixed race," I say.
"Wouldn't she be used to talking about—"
            "Yeah.
            Just not around Ethan, I guess."

Blond Ethan,
white as me.

Holly looks so bummed,
I think of how I could distract her,
look down at my old jeans,
remember something we used to do together,
say:

"Want to go shopping this weekend?"

She looks at my jeans too—then—

"Tomorrow?"
she asks.

A guilt wrinkle spreads through me.
I iron it down, smooth it out.

"Can't . . . meeting up with . . . Ellery. Sunday?"
She shrugs, agrees.

DYNAMIC TENSION
PHOTO CLASS #2, SATURDAY, OCTOBER 27TH
19 DAYS UNTIL IAA APPLICATION DUE

Ellery asks if she can meet Silas.
I say I'll ask him if we can all hang out.
I tell my parents (what I told Holly)
      I'm meeting up with Ellery.

In class, Fiona shows us a series
of time-lapse photographs:

             first, the moon in all stages circling the sky,
             next, planes taking off & landing,
             last, a planted seed blooming into a flower.

Then
dynamic tension.

How it can //intensify// a moment.

      She shows us two photos
      of the same bridge rising up for boats to pass.

One: shows the two sides separating in the middle
             perfectly symmetrical
Two: shows one side close-up
             like it's coming straight toward the viewer.

As she says this
Silas
             scoots his hand straight toward me
so close
we almost touch.

164

ENVISIONING

I pass Silas a note
asking if he wants to meet up
with some of my friends
after class.

With my mind-camera
I see

him and Ellery
laughing together,

his arm around my waist.
My head resting on his shoulder.

Kisses in between.

//Spin

spin

see//

BALANCING

On the way,
Silas & I hold each other's gloved hands.
His black leather,
mine green, knitted.

At the restaurant,
circus performers mural the walls.
Ellery's already at the table.
A tightrope walker
behind her.

Silas tells her he likes her
"Dolphins in Love" shirt.
She scans Silas's outfit,
says his hair matches his socks.

Taryn comes in late.
Kisses Ellery hard.

Silas grins, "That was fun."

"Really, dude?" Taryn says.

Both hands up, "Just a joke."

The tightrope walker wobbles.
My eyes glued to the wall,

        balancing,
I say: "Ellery . . . Silas is an artist—like us."
Ellery half smiles at me
asks Silas what it is he creates.

EXCUSES

Taryn doesn't talk much.

Eats her burger fast.
Makes an excuse
to go
before the rest of us
are done.

She leaves
without kissing Ellery.
"Not going to give you the pleasure,"
she says to Silas.

Once she's gone,
Ellery says,
"She's kind of intense,"
sips her milk shake.

"You think?" Silas asks.

I shift in my seat.

The tightrope walker
falls.

TUNNELING

After we leave,
           Ellery downtown,
me and Silas up,

I tell him,
"You know that wasn't cool,
what you said.
Lesbians aren't there
to get you off."

"Can't help it if I like kissing. All kinds of kissing."

Then he moves in on my neck.

His eyes are a tunnel,

and   I

       drive

       right

       in.

RELEVANCE

Silas brings me to his dad's house.
      Not far from the restaurant.
      Dad out at the movies,
      stepsister out with friends.

His room is what I expect:
      clothes on floor
      posters on walls
      a record player.

He puts music on,
leans me down onto the bed.

We kiss for a while
then he

puts his hand up my shirt.

      I push it down.

He puts it all the way up my thigh.

      I spring up,

"I love this song."

      "Me too,"
      he says,
      kissing my neck.

My eyes wander to a photo on the dresser
      —Silas with his mom and dad—

he looks about ten.

Then another of him and a girl.
Arms around each other.
The stepsister he mentioned.

"When did your parents get divorced?"

Silas laughs,
says, "I love it when you talk dirty."
"Seriously, I want to get to know you
better."

He pulls his arms off me.
I look him in the eyes.

He tells me it was a long time ago.
Just a typical divorce.

But then his eyes dart away.

He says
he doesn't remember them fighting.
Just remembers this feeling
of mismatch
when they were all together.
Remembers feeling they never fit.
That's when he started to draw.

I put his arms back
around me,
push him down
onto
the bed.

MATCHING

Sunday,
I hand Mom my homework
before she asks for it,
Holly and I escape, go shopping.

The gray fall sky
aches with dark clouds.

As we walk to Columbus,
I can still feel Silas's hands on me.
Silas
who is creative
      unique
        true to himself
more like me and Ellery
than Holly and her group.

Silas
who doesn't fit
with his family.

We enter the first store, which is
totally not my style.

But I try on
      boots
      fitted jeans
      a willowy shirt.

I look older, sexier.

Holly, new jeans and the same style shirt,
stands beside me in the mirror.

We don't look alike,

but in this one moment

just like
we used to love to do

we match.

PUSH/PULL

Holly starts walking into the next
                            fancier store—

"I don't want to go in there.
Too high-end,"
I say.

She rolls her eyes,   pulls me in.

                  We split up.
Me, the sales rack.   Her, the dresses.

The salesperson ignores me
but follows Holly everywhere,
          to the fitting room
              and back.

Once when that happened in middle school,
I stuck out my tongue at the salesperson.
Held Holly's hand.

Holly always looks so polished, put together.
Why would the salesperson—

               and then I see—

after Holly tries on a dress,
the salesperson
         smells it
before she puts it
back
on the rack.

INDIVIDUAL

Outside,
I say,

"That was messed up.
What the salesperson did?
After you tried on that dress?"

Holly looks at me,
says,

"Linc, seriously? That kind of thing happens all the time."

The sky opens.
It starts to pour

                        sheets of rain fall between us

we put our individual umbrellas up.

MEDITATIONS

Home,
later,
Mom says my homework
was better
than usual.
But
      in between sips of wine,
still a few harsh words:

"You better be working hard
on these other subjects
as much as history.

You're barely hanging on
in that school."

A narrow escape.
Push her words out of my mind.
Think of Silas's kiss.

I walk by Holly's room.
      She's cross-legged on the floor, eyes closed.

I go get a snack.
Come back.

      Eyes open, legs stretching.

I go in quietly.
All her sports trophies.
Flags from Brown, Yale.

My room still filled with
old pictures of us,
posters of Celtic symbols.

Hers about the future,
mine a tribute to the past.

When she still doesn't
acknowledge me,
I ask,

"What are you doing?"

She doesn't answer at first,
then turns to me.

     "It's kind of private."

Private like Silas
        my photo class
        IAA.

So I nod
  walk back out.

NEGOTIATIONS

Ten minutes later,
our old secret knock.

          3 times
          quick, quick, quick
     drumroll
2 taps.

I let her in.

"One for one?"
Holly says—

It's been so long
since we've traded anything real.

I nod.
"One for one."

     "I'm in therapy," says Holly.

     "I'm kinda seeing someone," I say.

DEFEATED

"You're in therapy? Why?
You always act like everything's fine."
"Linc,
      you think
      keeping it all together
      balancing everything
          is easy?

It's more like . . .
trying to block goals
from
a team
who's never lost
a game."

I try to picture Holly
in therapy.

Needing help.

Receiving it.

But all I see is someone
who blocks goal after goal
and hardly ever breaks a sweat.

THE WAY THE LIGHT BENDS

Holly says it was her idea,
she asked Mom if she could go,
had been feeling more anxious
than usual.

She says the therapist
suggested she meditate.
"I think it's helping—maybe."

Then tells me it's my turn.

I tell her about his blue hair
                his photography
                        how he looks at me.

"Where did you guys meet?"

        I think about Holly
                who I used to tell everything
                who now tells her secrets to Mom.

        It's too risky now
so I
    focus my eyes on the way
      her shadow cuts the wall

                the way the light bends
                the truth
and say—just half a lie—

        "I met him in the park."

PAUSES

I.
Holly says she's happy
                for me.

I smile,
but inside
my stomach sinks
with the weight of all
she doesn't know.

We never talked again about
Stefano—
       what he said,
       what I did.

But it's as if we've agreed
       to forget
       to move on.

For a moment,
it's almost as if we're drifting
       back to before
       back when we were
           younger
           closer.

II.
Before she leaves my room
       Holly turns and asks
       if I remember how
       on our trip to Ghana
       we toured all over

but never went
to the orphanage.

"I remember,
        why?"

She lingers in the doorway.
        Half in, half out,
touches the doorframe

            with one finger.

Then another.

        Like she might press her whole palm down.

        Like she might say.
        Like she might stay.

        Like maybe her stomach's sinking too.

Then
            she lifts her hand
                    her anchor
            back up

shrugs, says,
"No reason."

Guard back up.
Curtains drawn.

Together.
Apart.

EXPOSED

I.

We were 10.
The whole trip
Mom kept promising Holly
we would go

//but then//

she would try to distract her:
     shopping
     eating
     touring.

On our last day there
Holly asked about the orphanage
       again

Mom said she called
but there was a sickness going around,
she didn't want us

         exposed.

II.

We went back to the market,
tried to cheer Holly up.

Walked past people selling
     clothing
     fruit
     beads.

Women with baskets of yams on their heads
        another, mangoes
asking did we want any.

"Dabi," Holly said,
shaking her head no.

As Mom & Dad bartered for a drum,
Holly's soft dark eyes lit up.
She pointed.

        A woman selling batiks.

She looked so familiar
        so much like Holly.

Holly didn't have to speak,
I followed her lead.

III.
We each bought a shirt from the woman,
Adinkra symbols on them—
        Holly's, the symbol for loyalty.
        Mine, creativity.

The woman looked closer at Holly.

        "Wofiri hene?" ("Where are you from?")

        I looked at Holly too,
        uncertain what she would say.

She opened her mouth
        closed it

      opened it again
like a fish who'd been hooked.
Her eyes darted
down to her shirt
over at me.

Then
voice barely above
a whisper
she looked up and said:

     "We're from New York City."

ALMOSTS

Monday,
on the way to school,
Holly doesn't talk to me
about Ghana
but she does talk
student council drama.

The fall leaves glisten
          turn pink
as she chats & walks
close
next to me.

In chem,
Ellery sits beside me.
Her straw hair in braids woven
into other braids.

We get our tests back.
A 79! Almost a B!
The highest science grade
I've gotten all year.

I poke Ellery, show her,
she applauds silently.

After class, she asks
if she can talk to me about
      something.

"Sure, what's up?"

She says,
"Silas . . .
He was a little weird
on that double date.
Taryn thought so too."

I feel hot.
Tell her she just doesn't get him.
"He's really cool, I promise."
She nods,
asks if I like Taryn.
"Of course," I say.
        Though she's never taken time
        to get to know me.
Look back down at my grade.
Tell Ellery I need to go.

Wade through
the current of students,
look for Holly
to show her the test—

spot Stefano first.
His arm around her.
                I shift
                        with the current
            go back the other way.

POINT OF VIEW

Ellery's words
wind around my ribs.

I almost text her—to explain—

     instead—

     remind myself
     she doesn't know him
     the way I do.

True
he shouldn't have said
what he did,

but how many times have I
     said
     done something
I shouldn't?

*Can she judge his whole personality
based on one moment?*

We are all right.
We are all wrong.

It just depends on

who's behind the camera
who's in front
whose point of view
is looking.

LOOKING UP AT ME

Home after school,
Holly & Mom
are cooking black-eyed pea curry.

I read over my Artist's Statement again.
Knowing it needs more
but not sure what to add.

At least I'm on my way to a 2.7.

Over dinner Holly says she won a writing contest.

My turn to brag:
"I almost got a B on my chem test."

Holly smiles at me.
Dad tells me to say it louder.

"I got a 79!
My best test in science maybe ever?
An almost B!"

Mom says, "That's an improvement,"
then nothing more.

We finish our stew quickly.
Dad, Holly & I go out for Emack & Bolio's.
Holly & I get Deep Purple Chip.
No matter what's happening between us,
we always agree
it's the best ice cream flavor
in all of New York City.

QUESTION MARKS

Next day, in English,
we get our essays back.

Mine on defending Regan & Goneril's positions
in *King Lear*.

Maybe they betrayed King Lear for a reason.
Cordelia, always the favored sister.

Instead of my usual B, a C+.

My teacher says
my outside-the-box thinking was original like always.
But—

it seemed like I was in a rush.
I didn't have enough evidence.
My few text examples didn't quite fit
            my point.

            I reread my essay.
            It all makes sense to me.

How do people do it?
Balance all these subjects equally?

Was I in a rush?
Too focused on science? History?

I trace a line of question marks
with my finger
from hip to knee.

ATTENTION

That afternoon,
in my meeting with Mr. Chapman,
he congratulates me on my chem test.

But is less impressed
with my latest English essay—
says the teacher reported
my ideas were original
but my execution was sloppy.

"Success is all about
being exact,
being careful."

He squints his eyes at me.
      A stack of books land on his desk,
      wobble.
      Then stand perfectly still.
      In formation.

He asks about my history project.
I tell him how hard I've been working,
      how I'm actually excited about it.

He says he's glad to see me excited
about my education.
That today my GPA's at a 2.5,
tells me to keep it up.

      Books fly around the room
      in celebration.

FACES

In the school lobby,
Silas FaceTimes me,
says
he can't stop
thinking
    about us
    about me.

Says he wants to hang
again
soon.

His words mirror
my thoughts.

After,
I look at myself
through my phone's screen

look at
what he sees.

Smile,
flip my hair
at my reflection.

GHOSTS #2 & #3

Walk home from school
through the park.

Try to
>forget about
>my English paper,
>Ellery's words about Silas.

>Focus on the B+
>I need in history.

Pull my camera out,
zoom in
on my project,
>rough draft due in 6 days
>portfolio due in 16.

In the days of Seneca Village
NYC was a "city of contrasts."

>Downtown:
>>buildings
>>metal
>>cobblestone.

>Uptown:
>>streams
>>boulders
>>pastures.

Where I stand now was once

more country
than city.

Below me a puddle reflects
the light beaming off the sun
onto a can of soda.

Click &
capture
in one image:

         the can
         a building's edge
an apple core
a stump
a stone.

Then walk south—

The Great Lawn's haunted
by the ghost
of the Old Croton Aqueduct,
     the first dependable
     water source

     in all of New York City.

I get an idea.

Collect every empty
        water bottle

I can find.

       e   e
     k   a   v
   a   w a
M

of plastic
          now
overflowing grass.

Click/click/

contrast/
compare.

A PORTRAIT OF ME

I can capture
a symbol of the whole city—
in one frame, at once.

With my mind-camera,

I see my history teacher
nodding in approval
at my hard work.

I see the IAA teachers
looking at my photographs,

confident

in my vision

      a whole, complete
me.

I see my acceptance letter,
a future lined in photographs.

I smile into a future
portrait of myself.

BREATH IN

At home,
Dad asks if I want
Chinese food,
our favorite.

Holly says it's too fattening,
gives Mom indigestion.

They're both out,
so we go to The Cottage.

Before we leave,
Dad checks his wallet,
"Empty."

Checks the petty cash drawer.

"Huh, looks light."

His eyes turn to me.
I suck my breath in.

"Maybe Mom used some
to pick up the dry cleaning
the other day," I say.

Dad looks
back down to the drawer.

He waves it off.
"We'll use a card."
I let my breath out.

FORTUNES

Over dinner,
Dad asks me
how the history project
is going.

I tell him today,
I focused less on people,
more on the
environment.

Every curve and turn
in Central Park
so intentional.

So unlike
        the wilderness
it once was.

Dad nods his head vigorously
then we trade:
        my moo shu
        for his kung pao.

When we open
our fortune cookies,
he gets one that says:

All things are difficult before they are easy.

And mine:

Your ability to accomplish tasks will follow with success.

He grins, says my fortune has spoken,
this project will be
successful.

I try to smile back but
his prediction sinks in
      slow
like the grease sliding
down my fork.
Dad has no idea what kind of success
I'm working toward.

But they'll be so proud
when I get in,
they'll have to let me go.

All things are difficult before they are easy.

REACHING

Walking back,
Dad asks
how Holly seems
to me lately.

My stomach tightens but
I say "fine"
as I photograph:

a streetlight shining
on two different-colored
leaves
swirling
circling
reaching for
     each other.

They almost touch,
their veins almost meet.

Dad says he hopes
each of us
would talk to him
if something was wrong.
"I know," I say.

Then
I take one more photo
of the space between
the leaves.

SECRET LANGUAGE

Next day, during English,
Ellery has on her
"I Speak German.
What's Your Superpower?" T-shirt.

She passes me a note:
    What's up.
        Are we cool?

The air   between us   still **wobbly**
since she made that comment about
        Silas
since I lied about liking
        Taryn.

I lie again
write back
Nothing. Yeah we're good.

Pretend to read *Julius Caesar*.
She goes back to her work.
I turn pages but
it's more confusing to me than *Lear*,
looks like
gibberish.

While the teacher isn't looking
I text Silas instead,
tell him I have
                a secret.

He says
I like secrets.

Send a blushing emoji back.

He asks if I want to hang
tonight:
Halloween.

I type **yes.**
And then whisper it
again
out loud,
to myself.

NO DISGUISE

After school,
Ellery says
      she doesn't want things
      to be awkward
      between us.

      That if I'm happy,
      she is too.

Relief flows over me.

We go get donuts.

She asks if I want
to join her & Taryn tonight
at the *Rocky Horror Picture Show*.
She's going as Magenta.
Taryn, Frank-N-Furter.

I tell her thanks but I can't,
I'm hanging with Silas.
She nods,
asks if it's getting serious.

         Tell her no.
         "Well, maybe."

Tell her
sometimes I feel like
      a different person
when I'm with him.

"And that's a good thing?
That's what you want?"

Confusion passes through her
green eyes.

"Sometimes, yeah," I say.

We eat the rest of our donuts
in sticky silence.

MADE UP

Halloween night,
Holly knocks
on the half-open bathroom door
as I do my makeup.
She asks where I'm going.
If I want to go to some party with her.
I say thanks but I'm going out with Ellery.

Holly nods,
we line our eyes side by side.
Like when we would practice
in the mirror in middle school.

I'm in all black.
Silas and I are going
as photographers—
I should blend in
           with the night.

Dad, in the same old Dumbledore costume,
says he'll miss me passing out candy
      with him.
But he's also glad
I'm socializing more.

That he'll be fine,
there's a shipwreck special on
he's been dying to see—
"Go, enjoy."
I part ways with Holly,
vanish
into the night city air.

A MATTER OF PERSPECTIVE

Silas & I meet
just outside Gramercy Park.

We walk the blocks
around it.
He points out his school,
            the places he and his friends
        hang out.

Then
        we turn our cameras toward
                pirates
                superheroes
                fairies.
        A parade of little Ewok dogs.

        Trade lens filters.

        Drink "haunted chocolates."
        Hot chocolate with shots of espresso.

Silas tells me
Gramercy Park was just a swamp
before it became a park.

"Have you ever been inside?"
he asks.

        "Once, when I was eight.
        We got a key
        through Dad's work with
        the historical society."

(I don't tell him the escort kept insisting
Holly & I weren't really twins.
That Holly got upset.
How I stepped on his foot.
That Mom & Dad were horrified
but Dad was also proud
of how fiercely I loved
my sister.)

My sister.
Now off partying with her friends.
Dad at home watching shipwrecks.
Mom at work analyzing X-rays.
And me,
        with a boy none of them have ever met.

        So much more disconnected now
        than we were back then.

Or
I wonder:

have we always been this way and—

        just as an image can look different
                depending on your distance

                zoom out,
                zoom in—

        it is
                just the perspective that's
                                        shifted?

MELTING

We finish our drinks.
He throws out our cups.

The cold picks up.

Silas hangs on to the park's gate,
dangles his half smile
down on me then—
slowly—
pulls me into him.
I wrap my hands around his neck.

I am about to tell him
my secret

when he kisses me.

My thoughts melt.

                    We are
                    just lips

tasting
chocolate
and
each other.

CHARGES

Finally,
we come up for air.
I ask him if he's ever heard of IAA.
He says, of course,
best art high school in the city.

I tell him I'm applying,
          that's my secret,
and he's the only one

who knows.

He says that's great
but in a way that makes it sound
like he's not sure.

                    Lets go of
                    my hand.

Then he says his parents
would never let him apply.
Couldn't afford it.
Drags on his electronic cigarette,
pulls farther away.

                    Our bodies
                    no longer touch.

I ask him if he wants
to talk more about it.

He says there's nothing to say.

Some people can afford things,
        others can't.

Pulls out his camera,
gets quiet,
so I do too.
Try to ignore
the   changed
        charged
                air between us,
focus on images.

Make sure to shoot
not just people   inside the fence
                              of the park
but also those

                              outside of it.

Until I turn around
and realize
Silas isn't looking at any of them,

his camera's

    turned directly

                    on

                        me.

SLIDE AWAY

"Stop.
I don't like
photos of myself."

I cover my face.

      "But you're the most interesting subject out here," he says,

walks over,
touches my cheek.

The wind starts to blow.

         "Please? For me?"

I drop my hands
just below my chin.

         "Now smile,
         just a little.
            Yes! Look up.
            Just like that."

I smile   in spite   of myself

as all the
noise
light
colors
            slide away
until the moment's
           only ours to share.

TRANSFORMATIONS

At home,
Silas texts me a purple-tinted photo
of myself,

says he's been using Lightroom—

I look good in every color.

Surprised to see that
I do look okay, from that angle.
In purple.

I tell him
tonight was awesome,
but now I have
to study for my geometry test.

        I need at least a B-
        to pull up my grade in math.

I try to memorize
the theorems and rules
but every shape
    every angle
morphs into a heart.

INTERSECTIONS

During geometry
next day
the clock ticks loudly.

As much as I studied
how to calculate the angles
of

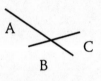

when I sit down
to take the test

they all look like
abandoned intersections.

My mind fills them
with freed carousel horses
    blue-haired people
    dancing.

SCATTERED

When I get home
I make a list of all my
Central Park photos.

      Should I order them north to south?
      Chronologically?
      Caption them with a "past landscape versus present"?
      How should I string together my history essay?
      How can I show the history of something that no longer exists?
      Honor Seneca Village as something that still matters?
      Is still with us?
      Say something significant?

I shuffle//
reshuffle//

                                  until the words
                                  and images

                  separate, float to the ceiling
                  and stick there.

                  I ask them to come back to me.
                  They don't.

In the end,
I go to sleep.

Wake up
to a pile
  a mess
      on the floor.
Everything   scattered.

SIGNIFICANCE

Next day
in history class,
Ms. Marshall says
she looks forward to seeing
the rough drafts
of our research projects
on Monday.

Says she wants an outline
      the start of the essay
          some "significant source material."

I know my images are significant.

But—

the best way to order them
      blend present with
          past

for the project
or the portfolio—

I still can't figure it out.

Fiona taught us about
white balance—
the feature of a camera
that blends light:

        natural with
        indoor with

fluorescent with
electronic.

With my mind-camera,
I press the
white balance feature
in my brain,
try to make it
all come together.

PREVISUALIZATION
PHOTO CLASS #3, SATURDAY, NOVEMBER 3RD
12 DAYS UNTIL IAA APPLICATION DUE
2 DAYS UNTIL ROUGH DRAFT DUE

I tell my parents
I'm going to the library.
That I concentrate better there.
They believe me.

      Ms. Marshall's mandate rings loudly in my head
            as I walk,
      the Artist's Statement looms over me.

          What is your vision?
          What truth are you trying to capture with your art?

Maybe Fiona can
help me find the answers.

In class
she gives a fancier name
to the mind-camera
concept:

      previsualization.

She says sometimes
images come out
just the way
you pictured.

Other times they
are a total

SURPRISE.

Silas looks at me
    lifts a finger
    presses it down
      on an invisible camera
    mouths "click."
My stomach flips.

SHOW MY EYES

Fiona gives us time in class
to print out photos,
then comes to each of us
individually
      looks at what we've been working on
the past few weeks.
A mid-session critique.

I show her
      children hand-clapping where the school used to be,
      water bottles on the Great Lawn,
      two leaves almost touching.

I explain how the park's ghosts haunt me
        how I want to give them a voice.

Fiona says she's impressed,
      young as I am,
to have such strong artistic vision.

I dare myself and
tell her about IAA.

Ask her if she'll write a recommendation.

She says absolutely—
her words
are a switch
and
every color in the room
brightens.

LAYERING EVERY MOMENT

Before we leave,
Fiona introduces me to color negative film.

    Shows me how silhouettes
    look dark when contrasted
    with an amber world.

Suddenly
    —a vision—
I can scan the photos I took on the old Nikon
    combine them digitally
        with images from my phone,

    overlay the two,
        present mixed with past.

    In the photo with the girls clapping
    I can add a school in silhouette.

    To the playground, an adjacent church.

    In the photo of Tanner's Spring,
    images of people gathering water.

So busy
    excited—
ideas churning,
images forming,
I barely notice
when Silas comes
behind me, says,
"Hey, class is over."

THE WHOLE SECRET

I text my parents
that I need more time at the library.
Don't wait for a reply.

Afterward—
we take a walk.

Silas is quiet.

Tell him
        I didn't share
my whole secret the other day.

Tell him
        I'm not sure
my parents would pay
for art school either.

They don't even know
        I'm applying.
He smiles
    holds my hand.

But doesn't say he thinks I'll get in.

Instead of asking
I pull him in toward
the park.

As we pass through,
Mariners' Gates
turn from stone to silver.

SUMMITING

We go to Summit Rock.
The highest natural point
in Central Park.
From there, you can see
where the Seneca Village homes
would've been.

I snap a photo.

      Remember
            the teakettle
            child's shoe
            roasting pan
      they found in the excavation.

      I could take a photo of household items
      superimpose them here, where the homes were.

      "Linc?"
            "What?"

      "I said, I like hanging with you."

Somehow I missed this moment
while envisioning another.
Turn,
focus on his bright-blue hair
against the pale-blue sky

      his full pink lips,
and as I kiss them
I say,   "Me too."

AN EXCEPTION

That night
I hardly sleep.
My mind dances with
Silas's lips,
my project ideas.

Sunday passes.
Mom comes in to
        review my work,
no wineglass this time.

            Old traditions
            made new.

I tell her
I don't think I did great
on my geometry test,
but I'm going to
ace my history project.

I wait

for what's familiar
to return

        for disappointment

        to bloom on her face.

        The glass to reappear.

But she tucks my hair behind my ear,
says,

"I can see you're trying, Linc."

Maybe she's trying
too.

It's enough
to keep me smiling
the rest of the day.

A gold star sprouts on my shirt.

SIDESTEPPING

Dad comes into my room
as I'm working,
brings me snacks,
says I seem so focused

lately.

And much more . . .
energetic.

He asks if there's
anything new going on.
Besides my project.

I stop working.

Try to picture
Silas coming over
like Stefano does.

But the image   is   foggy.

"No, not really," I say,
pushing it away.

"I have to go take pictures of a church."

He laughs, nods.

"Far be it from me
to distract a historian from her work."
He winks.

STITCHING

It's hard to capture
the whole church
in one image

to get the distance needed
from the other side of the block

so I do it in pieces.

The steeples.

The front door.

Try to use an
image stitching technique—
the combining of
multiple photographic images
with overlapping fields of view
to produce a panorama.

Maybe I could digitally
stitch them in.

My mind's going faster
than my camera can click.

OVERLAYING

Home,

I begin to do the overlaying.

Holly comes in
and lies down
on my bed.

She watches me work.

"That looks cool," she says.

I say thanks, ask her
what she's up to

but she's quiet
and I keep working.

"Oh, nothing, really,"
she says.

As she leaves
I realize
I didn't
look into her eyes
to see
if she was telling
the truth.

But—

I don't have time to wonder,

to go after her right now.

And—

when Mom asks

at midnight

if I am still doing homework
I'm not lying when I say

yes.

She gives me a head nod in approval,

doesn't tell me
to get to bed.

Click/click/stitch.

PRACTICALLY

Monday,
 Holly and I
walk to the bus stop together,
 just us.

She tries to talk to me
but my eyes keep closing
 at every red light that
 tells us to stop.

While we're waiting
she shows me
her rough draft
all printed out,
copies of the
suffragette petitions scanned.

Asks what I'm turning in.
Show her my owl-shaped hard drive.

I haven't done much writing
 yet
just a very basic outline
but I know the images
speak loudly.

They are strong,
 Fiona said,
and last night
I made them so much better.

I know they will   speak louder   than my words   ever could.

DELETE

In fourth period,
I hand over my hard drive
with a speeding heart,
then head to lunch.

Ellery tells me about Taryn
sleeping over this weekend,
and my fatigue sets back in.

I chug Coke,
try to pay attention.

On the other side of the caf,
watch Stefano glide up to Holly,
her head perched on his shoulder,
effortlessly,

Taryn now by Ellery's side,
sitting knee to knee.

Look at my phone,
text Silas: **miss you**.

Dare myself to send it.

And then,
deep breath in,
I do.

COULD HAVE BEEN

My phone buzzes.
Not Silas.
Mom.

Asking if I'll meet her at Holly's game later.

She shows up wearing scrubs,
a Ketchum High sweatshirt overtop.

Look down at my navy shirt,
orange sneakers.
"I guess I'm in school colors?"

Mom actually laughs
at my joke.
Places her hand on my back,
asks if I know what today is.

I think about it.

I don't.

She says her brother
would've been 45 today.
Before I can say anything back,
she says,
"Let's go get some pregame snacks."

As she hands me a pretzel,
my mind-camera focuses
on Roy.

Who would he have been at 45?
Would he have been here with us, cheering?

Mom is quiet,
her mind locked—continuous focus—
on her brother.

I try to picture his face
in hers.

Past/present/past.

SIDE-HUG

Dad meets us at the game.
Kisses Mom, side-hugs me.

We watch Holly block goal after goal.
Each time
someone shoots at the goal
                at Holly
my hand clenches my drink.
Mom cheers so loudly,
but sometimes I see her eyes go teary.

My mind-camera shifts focus
            zooms in on:
        our family.

We enter a photo gallery—

Mom beams as she sees
        my name on the wall
        my photographs on display.

She's so proud when she realizes

        finally
what I'm really capable of.

And she cheers
just as loudly
for me.

ARTIST'S STATEMENT FOR INNOVATIVE ARTS ACADEMY APPLICATION

Artists **are able to** express the world the way they see it. Oftentimes, they see things in unusual ways—sometimes they even see what isn't actually there but could be. My vision as a photographer is to show that there is more than one truth to any given moment. One example of this is how the past lives on in the present.

I have always felt better at expressing myself, more understood, through images. At a school like IAA, I believe I would be surrounded by others who could relate to this experience. Whether someone is sculpting, painting, acting, dancing, singing or taking a photograph, they are offering something to an audience. They are offering art and creativity. And through that art, the viewer is exposed to a new perspective.

I come from a family who sees academic achievement as the height of success. **It has only been recently that I've come to understand that there might be a whole group of people who actually see** my viewpoint as valid, essential, necessary. **Sometimes, we have a hard time seeing beyond what is right in front of us. Sometimes, our imaginations wither. As an artist, I hope to never lose this ability to imagine, and create newness, to own spontaneity, and to defy the temptation to look only on the surface. I hope I can always visualize the unseen and then make it come alive.**

In this portfolio, I have attempted to show the way the past of Central Park still lives inside its present. Central Park was once home to a place called Seneca Village. A settled community of outsiders, African Americans, immigrants from Ireland and Germany, all of them creating a home together, peacefully, in the wilds of New York City. All of them driven away by the wealthy Central Park buyers—people determined to make a beautiful park despite displacing a functional community. Through my portfolio I strive to keep this history alive.

I hope to keep finding places where, through art, I can help people discover what's been lost.

I hope to learn a lot more about respected photographers and the work that has come before my own. I know IAA can give me the tools and the confidence to move forward, and the humility to learn from the past.

PINGS

That night
I print out my Artist's Statement.
I print out the application: contact information, etc.
All that's left to do is sign it,
figure out the order of my portfolio,
write and refine captions for the images.

November 15th,
10 days away.

I focus on English homework,
reading *Julius Caesar*.

Then
my phone pings with a text—
          Ellery.

I text her back and realize
it's been hours since
I texted Silas **miss you.**

Just before bed
     finally   ping
he sends me an emoji

a boy and girl
kissing.
My heart   skips fast
                    ping, ping, ping
even as I try
to sleep.

STARE & MEMORIZE

Later that week,
geometry test
back.

63.

Nowhere near

A

B or

C.

When I studied,
things made sense.

I stared
I memorized
I understood what to do.

But now a red-marked paper
stares back at me,
        problems
                    still

not solved.

MONOTONY

In my weekly meeting
with Mr. Chapman,
he says it looks like
I might be failing math.

And my English grade has slipped
from a solid B to a B-.

He tells me it's important
that I keep my grades
front and center.

My GPA is back down to 2.4.
      I need to be careful.
      Keep working hard.

2.4 is not 2.7.
      Now I need more than a B+ in history.
      Now I need an A.

I look outside the window
  focus on something else
                  change the composition
                  see a new angle
anything to take me out of here
away from these words

but all I see are

endless windows
endless buildings
endless wintering sky.

SPEEDING UP

In history
on Friday
Ms. Marshall returns
our rough drafts,
says
many of us turned in
quite polished and
thoughtful work,
some really fresh ideas.

She looks directly at me.

I breathe a sigh of relief.

My breath quickens
like a train speeding up

my arms a field of goose bumps
as she
passes our projects back.

KEEP IN MIND

Along with my flash drive
Ms. Marshall hands me a note:

*Linc, this needs more words to be a history project. This is not an art
class. While I appreciate the way you took time with this, and I see
you are showing Seneca Village then inside Central Park now, I am
still not sure what you are saying about all of it. What is your thesis?
Please keep this in mind as you work on your final draft.*

The train grinds to a stop.
Goose bumps fall flat.

SUPERIMPOSE

Here's a thesis statement:
I'll never be good at this shit.

In the hall,
I pass Holly,
alone,
for once.

We lock eyes,
//caught//
in the same frame.

She asks me how I did.
I shake my head.

She calls for me
//to stop//
but I keep
walking right past her
to the bathroom.

                Out of her sight.

I don't want to hear
how hers is
already an A.

Instead I
      superimpose myself
           somewhere new
      text Silas:
Can you meet me after school?

POSING

Silas doesn't write back.

After school I head for the park,
take close-ups of bark,
find images as bleak as I feel.

Mid-shot
of a dead leaf
spinning in the air,
a buzz from Silas:

Where are you?

Twenty minutes later
he emerges through the trees
in a red-and-black-checkered coat.

I hold on to him
to keep from crying.
He asks if I'm okay.
I tell him not really.
Wait for him to ask why.

Instead:
"Do you want a lollipop?"

Says his mom found his pot stash,
she's straight-up mad.
These are all he has left.
Takes out a lolly
from his pocket.

Before I can say anything more
he says he wants
to take more pictures of me.

I take a quick lick
and then he's taking pictures—

me
on the swings

me
with just the sky

me
with the hot dog vending guy

me
striking a "fun and sexy" pose

me
pretending.

Really
I just want to talk
      want Silas to tell me
           everything is going to be fine

but it feels so good   to not be me
to just

                      lick lollies & forget
so I pose
and pose
and pose.

SUDDENLY, EVERYTHING

We sip each other's sodas.

I ask if he always drops
whatever he's doing
to come to the park.

"Only for cute and talented girls," he says.
His stepsister was annoying him anyway.
Picking fights.

"She's pretty, your stepsister."

He looks at me quizzically.

"The photo? You and that girl ... in your room?"

       He's quiet for a minute.
       Then says
       oh, no, that's an ex.

"Oh."

       I look at him then,
       this guy, my first kiss.

"So how come
you still have her picture up?"

       He says she's still a friend.

"How long were you together?" I ask.

"I don't know.
A year or so."

Suddenly, everything   feels   wrong.

The trees are on fire.
          The half-moon glows in the afternoon sky.
                    What was once a village is now a park.

I tell him I feel sick—
leave him standing there—
run all the way home.

ZOOM

Back in my room.
Try to clear away
the image in my head—

Silas belonging
with another girl.

I run my finger
along Roy's camera.

Ask it to
give me
a new view.

Photos
that need an essay, words.
My history project
that needs cohesion, a clear viewpoint.

My mind-camera
shooting recklessly,

I force myself to quit

                shifting

                                focus

and just/stop/click

zoom in.

SOPHOMORE RESEARCH PROJECT
Linc Malone, US History, Ms. Marshall

"Searching for Seneca Village": Snapshots of Central Park's Present & Past

When you think of Central Park, you think of the carousel, the reservoir, Belvedere Castle. You think of the most beautiful, peaceful part of this crowded, busy city. But—can we assume just because something appears beautiful that it is?

Central Park might be beautiful, but its beauty is tainted. Before Central Park, there was Seneca Village. From 1825 to 1857, in the upper west side of the park, Seneca Village (and the neighboring "Pig Town") was home to African Americans. After 1840, Irish, running from the Potato Famine, and German immigrants lived there too. These people coexisted peacefully, worked the land and raised their children next door to one another.

Seneca Village even had an integrated church, during a time when most of the city lived segregated lives. That is, until wealthy buyers bought the land and forced them all out.

But what if people who lived in Seneca Village, in the neighboring villages, had had more power? What if they had had the means to stop the buyers? Would Central Park have been built somewhere else? Somewhere people weren't already making their own peaceful lives? My photographs show how Central Park is still haunted by this history, despite modern appearances.

In my photographs, you will see where the churches, schools, homes used to be. If you use your imagination and squint, you can find the peaceful village again.

Through the course of this project, I learned that history is made up of a million stories. It all depends on whose you choose to see. To the builders of Central Park, the story here is one of opportunity. To people who enjoy it now, one of the most amazing parts of New York City. Some would even say its heartbeat. To the people who were bought out? A loss, maybe even a tragedy.

History is like colors in photographs. It is different depending on your perspective, the angle of your viewpoint. When people say color, what they really mean is light. For every photo, you can add more light and watch the colors change. Darken it, the colors shift again.

There's no one truth.

Only stories. And light.

I print my essay.

Then work on the captions
for my photographs.

Make sure to
name each place today
and what existed then.

> Sheep Meadow (filled with plastic water bottles).
> Once the Old Croton Aqueduct.

> The green field at 85th Street.
> Once the homes of Seneca Village.

> Tanner's Spring.
> Once the site of cooking, laundry.

For every ghost image, a caption.

And then I print out
the Seneca Village map.

Mark a number where I took every photo.

I look down at my desk.
My schedule,
all my important dates.

Only 6 days until the application is due.

Almost done.
Just need to print a few more photos
at the Center.
Pick up the rest I've already made.

I picture my A+
          my acceptance letter to IAA
surrounded by gold stars.
Mom, Dad, Holly watching them—
                    watching me—
glow.

Imagine it
then make it
real.

PACING

When Dad gets home,

I show him the note from Ms. Marshall.

But then
I tell him everything
about
my new thoughts
and ideas.

He reads my essay.

He says these ideas are just what history is about.

But then he sounds like my teacher:

"You just need to slow down—

guide the reader—

    thought by thought
    example by example.

Right now, it feels a bit vague.
You need to build an argument
to persuade the reader."

As he tells me to slow down,
my excitement
s l o w s too.
A running faucet

dialed back
to just a drip.

When I'm taking pictures,
the click of the camera matches my
mind's quick movements.

Sitting down with the essay,

the ideas aren't the hard part.

It's the planning
it's the proving

restating what you've already stated
requoting what other people have already said.

Drip.

Drip.

Drip.

All I want is to
get into the air
get my camera out

swallow images whole.

Click/

click/
wish.

WHAT'S MISSING

Silas texts
a photo of his desk.

The picture of his family is still there.
But the one of him and his ex?

                              Gone.

I know he's trying to show me
he's sorry
but

                    things feel off.

I'm not sure what
to say back

            so for now

I stand on my chair
take photos of my own
cluttered desk

no framed pictures,
just endless papers

                    images without captions

and I don't reply.

TRAILS OF LEAVES

Dad asks me
to help him with dinner.
Mom & Holly
will be home soon.

With a knife,
I carve flowers out of tomatoes,
starfish from red peppers.

Dad asks if I'm sculpting
or cooking.

By the time Mom & Holly get home,
I haven't even washed the lettuce.
Rush to get it done,
trail of leaves at my feet.

At the table,
Mom says she's thinking of taking
two weeks' vacation this summer.
Something she rarely does.
She wants to take us to Ireland,
where most of both
her and Dad's families are from.

Holly does that thing where she
moves her lips from side to side.
Cracks her knuckles.

Seems more anxious than excited.

Mom's phone buzzes,

she gets up to check it.

When she comes back,
she looks hard at me, says,
"Linc, your advisor emailed.
We need to talk."

I look down, away
from Holly's pitying look,
back to
my pepper starfish
now drowned in dressing.

BLANK PRINT

Holly excuses herself.
Mom says,
"That was an email from Mr. Chapman—
      you're failing math,
           in chemistry too you've fallen behind,
      your English essay: the worst of the year.
Creative but rushed."

I explain how
I've been working hard on history,
on every subject really.
How she's seen me.

Dad backs me up.

"Well, when are we going to see it pay off?" she says.

I sit still
    a print
    in a solution bath
waiting to develop
something worthy of display.

Mom looks at me
like I might have something else to say.

When I don't,
she gets up,
walks away.
I stay still
& blank.

She's angry.

Again.

Will she even let me out of the house?

I need to get to class tomorrow,
I need their scanner and printer to finish my project & portfolio.

Think quickly.

Holly trusted me
with her secrets.

We're sisters.
Knock on her door using
our secret knock
     3 times
          quick, quick, quick
     drumroll
     2 taps.

When she opens,
I push my way in,
close the door behind me.

Before she can open her mouth
I say:
"Holly, I need a big favor."

TRANSPARENCY

"So—
remember that guy I told you about?"

She nods.

I tell her
we're in a fight,

how I need to see him tomorrow.

I don't mention
class—
the real reason
I need to go.

Then:
"Mom's so mad
I'm scared to ask to go out."

Holly sighs,
        sounding exasperated like Mom,
says fine, she'll say we're doing
some early Christmas shopping.

Surprised how quickly Holly
comes up with a lie too.

I just hope her eyes—
        always transparent
        showing the truth—
don't give us away.

A BLOCK AWAY

Next day
Mom won't even look in my direction
but she buys Holly's lie,
tells us she and Dad are
going to go out shopping too.

Outside the wind bites cold.
First snow of the season lightly falling.

Holly walks close beside me.
Asks why we're fighting.

I say he has a long-term ex
he didn't tell me about.
They're still friends.

Silas meets me on Amsterdam,
where I asked him to be,
leaning against a building,
vaporizer in hand.
I point him out.
Thank her.

"Hope it works out," she says,
but I see the flash of concern
      in her eyes as I

                    go.

REPLACING

Silas, dusted with snowflakes.
    Blue hair,
    growing out a bit.
    Replacing itself
    with brown.
Tell myself to forget about the ex.
I reach out to hug him,
  lose myself in his tall frame.
He gives me a smoky kiss.

I pull away quickly.
Don't want to be late for class.

He asks who that was.
"My sister—
she's adopted."
Suddenly realize
how much he doesn't yet know about me.
      "Why didn't you introduce me?"

We walk down the block
        in silence soft as snow
as I realize
it never even occurred to me
to do so
so I lie and say, "She was in a rush."

Then:
    we push in the door
    to the Center.
He leads me in.

IMAGES
PHOTO CLASS #4, SATURDAY, NOVEMBER 10TH
5 DAYS UNTIL IAA APPLICATION DEADLINE

Before class,
I take my prints
from my folder.

Look at the original images,
the ones without the ghosts stitched in.

I ask Fiona:
"Can I print some new ones during class?"

She nods yes.

Fiona says she's finished
with my recommendation,
already sent it in.

With my mind-camera
I see someone at IAA
reading it, smiling.

Just then I get a text
from Holly,
How long will you be?
Give me two hours, I write back.

After my critique
I'll get my prints
then duck out early.
Switch the ringer to vibrate,
put my phone away.

MINUTES LEFT

Fiona teaches us
about juxtaposition.
How photographic subjects
work to emphasize
or deemphasize
each other.

For example,
        an image of a bike wheel
        at the edge of a photo
        of a carousel
                might emphasize
the circular motion of both.
        Or how a live horse
        next to a carousel
                might make the viewer
                think more about
        imitation versus
        reality.

Minutes pass.

I keep one eye on the clock.

I print doubles of my photos
then it's critique time.

One classmate
shows us photos of bubbles
        in banks
        tollbooths
        convenience stores.

Bringing childhood into mundane spaces, she says.

I feel myself   floating too,

      then see Silas frowning.

Clearly he thinks they're cheesy.

Another person is up.
These photos are of animals.

From the park,
      the zoo,
      the sky.

They are harder to get lost inside.
Just lots of animal eyes.

I watch the minute hand move.

Four more critiques.

In between
Fiona teaches short lessons
relevant to the artist's work
until finally
it's my turn.

The ceiling opens up,
sky pours through.

HISTORY UNSEEN

My heart flips.

I show my prints.
Explain what I'm trying to do.

Someone says beautiful,
          another so cool,
                    a third visionary.

My heart swells.

I stop looking at the time.

Fiona says I've done
a great job with the
perspective and juxtaposition.

Then one person asks
if we need to know the history
to understand my photos.
My stomach sinks.
Would Mom ask that too?
Maybe this project
is worthless.

I glance at Silas
who's beaming at me
and I get the courage.
I say:

"No, I don't think so.

Whether or not you know the history,
you can see the layering of the images
is significant,
telling a different story
than the one that appears
on the surface."

Then Silas backs me up, says:
"Really makes you think.
Showing how many things exist at once."

"Thank you," I mouth.
In that moment,
I see us
wrapped in the woods
limb to limb

branch to branch.

WITHOUT A CHANCE

More critiques left
          including Silas's
but I have to go—

already twenty minutes late.
But I couldn't walk out
on my own critique.

Holly will be okay.

Whisper "sorry" to Silas, the class—
gather my things quickly,
rush to rejoin the world.

Outside in the cold,
all my prints in hand,
racing,
beaming with the class's positive words.

Turn on Amsterdam,
rush to close the gap
between me and where
Holly is waiting,
spy—

                    a fair-skinned woman
                    with auburn hair
                    in a low ponytail,
                    big brown down coat.

It takes a second for my brain
to catch up with my eyes

but when it does
I realize
the person standing
on the corner is

     not Holly,

it's

                  my mom.
     My heart jumps into my throat.
     I freeze.

PROPELLING

Mom grabs me by the arm
and almost pulls me home.

   I hang on to my photos
desperately
as her anger propels us forward,
cuts through the wind.
   She stops
like she just noticed
what I'm holding.

Grabs them from me.

               "Is this what you've been doing?"
               "Every Saturday? After we told you no?"
               "So selfish!"

               "What were you thinking?"

                         she yells
                         as we continue down the street.

The wind rushes past.

                         What were you thinking?
                         The question repeats.
                         But this time
                         it's me who asks.

The air
cyclones.

Stupid/
stupid/
stupid.

And then repeat.

LOCATING

Holly hardly   looks at me
when I get home.

I can hardly look   at her
        either.

Then
I take out my phone.
Dead.
Shit.

        What happened?
        I don't get the chance to ask her.

My parents need answers
        need to know
NOW:
        How long have I been lying?

As angry as they are,
I am almost used to it by now.

Mom looks expectant, mad.

But—

Dad looks hopeful
like I might have a good explanation.

        It hurts much more.

I take a deep breath.

Tell them the truth about the class.
How I paid for it.

Then it isn't Mom

        but Dad

who starts yelling.

Click/

click/

switch.

AFTER DREAMS

Dad says
my behavior
      is unacceptable.

I tell him I'm just trying
to go after my dreams.
      "Don't I deserve to try?"
      "Don't my dreams mean anything to either of you?"

But he says I'm being selfish.
And childish.
That they cannot trust me.
That they are so disappointed.
That I'm grounded again.

Mom asks:
Was it worth it?

So I don't tell them about IAA.
How the Center was a means
to get me there.

It would only make things
worse—

      Dad's harsh words
      Mom's icy looks
         make that clear—
so I say the only thing left to say:
      another
      flimsy
      "sorry."

STRETCHING

I walk into Holly's room
without knocking
this time.

She's in downward dog.

       "How could you do this to me?"

       She finishes her stretch.
       Moves into plank.

Calmly says, "I was worried."

Her calm makes me angrier.

       "I would never rat you out like that!"

She moves into a cross-legged position.

"Look, I'm sorry.
I waited ten minutes
on the street for you.
It was freezing.
I came home
and Mom was here,
insisting that I explain why
I came back without you—
you know how she can be!
Besides, that guy you were with . . .
I did *not* get a good vibe."

       "This is not about him. It's about me!

Going after what I want and
everyone else just getting in the way and
ruining things.

And you don't know anything about him!
Or me!"

I leave her as she shrinks further into herself.

Child's pose.

IN ORDER

Slam my door,
lock it.
Plug in my phone.

I have
the prints from class,
some of them even multiples.

Who cares if I'm grounded.
I can
still make my portfolio.

Glue
captions to the photo backs.

Put
my photos in order of the map.

Forge
my parents' signatures.

How much more trouble could I get in now?

Check
the shipping places open this time of night.
Find
three on the Upper West Side.

I've got nothing   left   to lose.

POUNDING

After Mom & Dad go to bed,
Holly on the phone, laughing,
I sneak
      down into the kitchen
            rip
            a check from Dad's checkbook
            for the application fee, shipping
     then head out
         into the night

wade through
the city that never sleeps.

Every step echoes
          pounds
into my head
my mother's words
my father's too.

Every piece of litter
     every "don't walk"
screams and scowls,

"Selfish."
"Childish."

I ignore them all,
carry my application to a 24-hour UPS.

Dare myself.

Mail it.

WORTHINESS

I walk and walk and walk.

I can't go home yet.

Think of texting Ellery
but I don't have
the energy to explain
everything.

At least there's
one person who
knows enough already

and who
really gets me
really sees me.

He said my images
make the viewer think.

Was it worth it?
my mom asked.

Every step I take
is a
yes
yes
yes.

I text him I'm coming his way.

DRIFT & HOLD

Silas

blinks twice
when he sees me on the street.

Snow drifting at his feet. d

e

He doesn't ask questions, h

c

t

e

r

t

s

t

u

just holds his arms o i fall right in

u

t

s

t

r

e

t

c

h

e

d

FORGETTING

Looking into his eyes,
I find the words.

I tell him how
      I lied
      stole money
      to pay for the class.

My sister ratted me out.

I tell him I just mailed in my application to IAA.
Screw my parents.

Tells me he had a shitty night too.

"What happened?"
I ask.

But he doesn't say
      why
      what
         or who.

And like he's read my mind,
he says now that we're

        //together//

the rest of it doesn't matter.

A HALO

He backs me
into a street alley.

       If I took his photo
       now

       it would be a portrait:
       the light in back of him,
           a halo.

He says forget about your parents—

       everyone can see you're talented.

He tells me I am beautiful,

a visionary,

       pulls me closer.

"As beautiful as your ex?"
I ask.

He doesn't respond.

"Have you had a lot of girlfriends?"

       "Linc," he says,
       "I'm into *you*."

I feel it in his body.
I let myself believe him.

FLASHES IN THE DARK

We go into a random movie.
There's hardly anyone in the theater.
                The lights go down.

We don't see much of anything,
       just each other.
I've never had anyone touch me
           where he does.
Bra undone, zipper down.
Here, in a theater.

Feels like I'm inside a movie myself.

I feel shy about touching him,
     he shows me how.

His eyes close.
His face glimmers.

                I ignore whatever story is being told.
                 Ignore my phone
              when it lights up
              with text after text.
Power it down
without reading.

Say yes <u>to him</u>.

            The movie screen's images
                the only flashes
                pulsing
                in the dark.

FRAMING

SOMETHING INSIDE

After the movie,
      Silas says
he has to deal with "some things."
We'll see each other soon.

I ask him if we are, like,
exclusive.

      "Sure," he says back.

I smile.

We kiss goodbye,
but I keep that warmth inside

as I pass

      each person
      car
      flashing light

all the way back
uptown.

DOUBLE MOMENT

I walk inside
    quietly,

almost jump when I see
    Holly.

She says she covered
    for me

didn't tell anyone
    I was gone.

Is that supposed to make me
    forgive her?

I tell her I'm still
    mad.

She says she didn't
    have a choice.

      Couldn't she have chosen to wait just a little longer?
      Couldn't she have chosen not to tell Mom?

"You don't get it.
Mom & Dad are different

with you—

they let
    you do

just what
  you want
  what you love."

She nods, says,
    "But they don't know
everything I want."
Tears hover in her eyes.

I can tell
    she wants me

to ask
    what she means
but tonight
    I don't want to.
    I want to keep
        me and Silas
    our shared night
alive.

So:
    I go to my room
      climb into bed
    eyes wide open,
    I watch a slide show.
    No angry mother
    no disappointed father
    no sad sister, just
    Silas & me

    kissing

over and over and over again.

LAYERS

The next morning,
Mom doesn't let me sleep in.

She says she knows
my final history project
is due in a week.

I don't need her to
remind me.

Reread
revise
polish
          my essay

          try to prove   point by point
that the expulsion of the inhabitants

was a tragedy.

That the community is one
that deserves

                              remembering.

I can't know the suffering
of an African American
owning land for the first time
then being robbed of it.
An Irish immigrant
trying to make a new home

in a foreign country, not their own.

I can't know how that kind of   displacement
feels.

But I do know what it's like to glimpse
a sense of belonging

                       just to be tossed right
                       out-

side of it.

EVERY ANGLE

Monday
Silas texts that he'll miss me
in class this week.
I text him
you and me both.
Send a crying emoji face.

In history class,
Ellery
shows me
her outline
        she's printed out
        and then ~~crossed out,~~
                written over.

Other students mumble
that this project
is making them crazy,
that they don't have enough
        source material,
that they know they're
        going to fail.

Later,
at home,
I look down at my own.

        This project
        these photographs
        this history.

I stand up.

Move across the room.

I look at my images from
every angle
the way they tell a story.
But whether sideways or upside down
my work

doesn't make me feel crazy—
it is the only thing that grounds me.

SNAPSHOT

All week I
study
do homework
keep my head down
     my GPA up
focus on
     English quiz on *Julius Caesar*
     chemistry problem sets
     geometry too
rework my essay for history.

Ignore texts from Ellery.

Now, Saturday—
during the time
I'm supposed to be
     in photo class #5—

Mom & Dad demand
I organize the overstuffed hall closet.
They say that in addition to being grounded,
I will do chores to make up for
the stolen money.

Fiona,
Silas,
all my classmates
making art

     as I sort loose wrapping paper,
     hunt for matching gloves.

A box labeled "Roy Memorabilia"
—the one that held his camera—
makes me stop.

I make sure no one
is around before I
open it up.

Inside:
a small sketchbook
full of
hands,
faces,
buildings

a card
      "My dearest Cynthia sister, Where would I be without you?
      Let's live forever together.
      Happy Birthday, your dearest Roy brother"

cassette tapes
      The B-52s, The Police

a snapshot of teenage Roy
      and a friend in front of
a place called Tower Records.

When I hear Mom's footsteps coming
I stuff it all back into the box.
Spend the rest of the day
ordering and reordering
my source material
—every photo and caption—
figure out the story I want to tell.

WATCH

Monday,
my project is done.
    It is big.
The words next to
the images
     small.

I feel people

watch me

       cradle the folder
           through the entrance to school,
     hold it close to my chest
         as I walk down the hall.

          In history,
          Ms. Marshall reaches out
           when I hand in my project.

      I've never been this proud
      of schoolwork before.

My hands shake

as I

let
go.

AT LEAST

Mr. Chapman says
what I already know:
a lot is riding on my history project.

I tell him I'm not through
trying—

with history, yes,

but also math
              science
              English.

       2.7 GPA *preferred.*

       I have to get into IAA.

On my way out
of his office
I turn on my mind-camera,
view its slide show:

       I am in a photography room
       in a new school
       surrounded by kids
       like me
       printing, critiquing, scanning

click, click, click.

WHAT BELONGS

Thursday is Thanksgiving.

As soon as break begins,
Dad has me clean out the fridge
in preparation
to make room for the turkey.

My tasks:
      Pull everything out.
      Wipe down each shelf.
      Wipe down every jar.
      Check each expiration date.
      Put everything back that hasn't
            spoiled.

He doesn't look at me
as he preps food in the kitchen

but I still can't help but think
      if Dad were inside my head
      if he could see my mind-camera
he would understand
that I've been working hard
         working toward something real.
That my dreams are something worth

                         hanging
on to.

That he shouldn't
give up on me.

SENDING

That night,
Silas wishes me
a happy early Turkey Day,
asks
       how I'm doing

       will he ever see me again
           now that I won't be in
           photo class?

       Now that I'm eternally grounded?

I tell him of course he will.

He asks if I can send him a photo
of myself

for the time in between.

I have a feeling he wants
something sexy—

I send him

my bare shoulder,
the end of my hair
crossing over it.

He sends me back
a picture of

just his lips.

IN THE AIR

Thanksgiving,
Ellery FaceTimes me.
Been a while since we've really
talked,
she says.

Between school and relationships.

Now she's in Savannah.
She says being there on Thanksgiving is fine
but nothing compared to
    St. Patrick's Day when
      they dye the river green.

Says she visited the school where her parents met:
    Savannah College of Art & Design.
"Maybe one day, we can go there for college.
We can be in art classes for four years
together."

      I tell her nothing would be better.

Picture myself there with her
instead of stuck in my room,
alone.
We are standing near a green river

              painting colors in the air.

    The whole city cheering us on.

OVERTAKING

The Monday after break,
after a perfectly cooked turkey
     by Holly & Mom
after exchanging only
     a few words with either of them

after hours
     days of

       doing chores
       or homework,

Ms. Marshall
hands back our reports.

Linc,
Your photographs are beautiful.
However, as I said before, it seems as though you have let the visuals
guide your project, and as a result, they manage to really overtake
the content of your argument. I can tell how hard you worked on
this, and I appreciate your effort here and your passion, but I still
think you have missed something fundamental on how to organize
an argument. This reads more like a creative nonfiction piece than a
history essay. Please see me after class and we can talk further.

C+

CLARITY

I race out of class
without a word to Ms. Marshall.

I put everything I had
        so much of

            myself

    into that project.

But now,
walking the hall,
lugging my prints,

            Ms. Marshall's words ringing in my ear

it has never been clearer:

I cannot stay
I do not belong
I have to get out of
                    here.

NOTHING & EVERYTHING

As I walk down the hall

      the lockers shake
               rattle
               tremor.

My mind shoots out the question:
Is there any way now I could get a 2.7 GPA?

But then—

the sight of
Ellery crying
pulls me back
into this moment.

I follow her
down the hall into
the bathroom.

"What happened?" I ask.

She says
after she got home from Savannah,
she and Taryn
got into a huge fight.

"It seemed like it was about nothing,
but then I guess it was about everything."

I circle my arms around her.
She cries and cries.

LOOKING DOWN

She says there's no way
she's going to class.

Can I come with her?

                    //Cut?//

I look down at my project.
My C+.

Look at my best friend,
who has believed in me.
No matter what.

It doesn't take me long to decide.

I follow her   out.

PASSES

We go to Ellery's house.
      Her parents out at work.

She cries more.
To distract her,
I show her my photographs,
then she's
crying
about how beautiful they are.

"I applied to IAA."

      "The art school? Your parents let you?"

"They don't know."

Her eyes get wide
she squeezes my hand
      passes me a spoonful of peanut butter
in chocolate sauce.

We face the TV,
pass the spoon
      back and forth,
turn the volume up.

NOT SURPRISED

When my phone rings,
I know what it means.

I've been caught.
    Again.

No getting out of it this time.
I pick up.

Dad says
we have an appointment
        me
        him
        Mom
with everyone at Ketchum in the morning.

I need to come home.

~~~Right away.~~~

I tell him there were reasons.
I promise.
This time he'll agree
my behavior was justified.

He says I seem to have
so many excuses lately.
We will talk more later.

I hang up
watch myself vanish
into Ellery's mirror.

BLURRY

Before I leave,
Ellery gives me a long hug.
Tells me she's sorry
she made me cut.

I tell her no,
we did it together.

A long walk home,
still lugging my photos, my essay.
Text Silas
I messed up.

Dad meets me
at the front door.
Before he can say anything
I tell him

       after all that work,
           a C+.

       And Ellery needed help.

       I followed my gut.

He doesn't speak at first,
just closes the door behind me.
Takes off his glasses,
rubs his eyes.

Then,

"I'm sorry about your grade
but that doesn't excuse you cutting school.

I'm worried about you, Linc.
Worried about the choices
        you've been making lately."

This didn't feel like a choice,
I want to say.

It felt clear,
necessary,
right,

just like when I shoved
Stefano

        enrolled
                in photo class

        sent in my application.

I look down at my hands
try to see each finger individually

but   all   they   do   is   blur.

SWALLOWS

Lying in bed,
waiting for Silas to text back
   heart rushing
      unable to sleep
      listen to the cars
      picture myself jumping into one
         riding it into the night

            away
              from what will happen tomorrow
            away
              from a life that doesn't feel like my
              own.

I dream until
I hear Mom come in late

she and Dad murmuring

through the wall.

Then she opens my door

      mouth puckered tight
      eyebrows scrunched

if she sees me
see her

she doesn't say.

Just turns and leaves.

TIME-LAPSE

All four of us are silent
in the cab
on the way to school.

The rush of the city   flies   by
          faster than it should.

I am trapped
in a time-lapse
photograph.

As Mom, Dad & I walk

              out of the cab

              down the street

              through the door,

as Holly leaves us for Stefano,

I hang my head low,
walk past all my choices,

              in s l o w – m o t i o n

down the hall.

FADING

We sit in the principal's office.

> Mom still hasn't looked at me.
> Dad's hand rests on her knee.
> Me, alone, in a chair.

The principal doesn't waste any time,
says

my time at Ketchum

is <u>over</u>.

Between my low math and science grades
academic probation
recent suspension
and cutting school yesterday,
they have no choice but to **expel** me.

No one says anything about all my hard work
my attempts to improve.

The room becomes a box.
All the sides fold in.

Everything fades to black.

AS, IN, STILL

I tell them:

I'm sorry
for being such a disappointment

       as we leave the room
       as we get the books from my locker
       as we walk back down the hall

       in the cab back home
       in through the gates
       in the foyer of our house

but Mom

       still doesn't speak a word to me.

GHOSTS #4

All day
I
am
a
ghost.
I
move
from
room
to
room
but
no
one
talks
to
me
knocks
on
my
door.
The
house
        so
            quiet
I
wonder
if
I
have
actually
disappeared.

TUMBLEWEEDS

Shame
fear
    keep
tumbling in like
weeds
in a desert.

Stuck. Sweating.

I am so stupid

comes first, then:

*Does getting expelled
mean I have no chance
of getting into IAA?*

*Could my portfolio still
be enough
to win them over?*

Hope is thin,
a mirage of water.

Stupid, stupid, stupid.

The weeds keep rolling in.

On a loop.

No sign of rain.

APPARITION

Ellery sends me "I'm sorry" GIFs
to try to make me laugh.

I send her back a laughing emoji
but don't even crack a smile.

Silas finally texts, says,
Hey, you ok?
I ask
        if he's ever been expelled.

He says no
but almost.
        I ask him how he feels about
        having a girlfriend who has.

He says he can't wait
        to celebrate with me
        when I get into IAA.

It isn't the answer to my question
        but it makes me feel
        like I haven't

        vanished completely.

VIRTUALLY

Later that night—
Dad comes in.

Says I'm joining a cyber school
until they can figure
something else out.

I tell him maybe I already have.

I tell him I never belonged at Ketchum.
That I know it was wrong to steal money for the photo class
but I only did it because it's somewhere I belong.

He says he doesn't want to hear it.

You lied.
<u>*Stole.*</u>
Betrayed our trust repeatedly.

So I don't tell him the rest.

But Dad's not finished.
He says he knows I'm sorry
but sometimes words mean less than actions.
That I need to <u>show them</u> I'm sorry,
            <u>show them</u> I can do better.
"Can you do that?"
My mind flashes again to IAA—
        that's the place for someone like me
                <u>a place</u> I can succeed
                <u>a place</u> I can make them proud
so I say to him, "Yes, I can."

Holly knocks quietly.

      Asks if I'm okay.

I stay silent.

      "Can I see your project?"

"Whatever. I guess,
if you feel like it."

      I know she's only asking because
      she feels sorry for me

      because she feels bad about ratting me out,
      robbing me of my dreams.

But she looks through each photo, delicately.

      "They're so beautiful,"
      she says.

      If I wasn't disappearing, I might almost smile.

IN HER HANDS

I go to the kitchen
for some water

        see Mom
        head in her hands,
        Dad beside her.
        Empty drinks on the table.

It isn't even Sunday.

They don't say anything

               as I pass

      but I know

            I am

        the object
        of her grief.

Click/
click/
vanish.

IN, OUT

Thursday morning,
they're all around the kitchen table.
Getting ready for school and work.

Dad talks logistics
    tells me
          he emailed me
          the log-in information,
          I'm all signed up
          that they will receive notifications
          when I log in,
          hand in work,
          log out.

They'll be keeping watch.

Then
Mom says the first words
she's spoken to me
since expulsion Tuesday:

"We've set up a drop-cam.
We'll be able to see you.
No TV."

The door closes,
only Holly waves goodbye.

I give the finger
to the drop-cam.
It flashes red at me.

CYBER SPACE

Before I log in,
I text Ellery,
ask her if going to school online
makes me a robot.

She writes back
again,
she feels so bad.

She's apologized so many times.

I tell her again it wasn't her fault.
Quote my dad,
"We are our choices."

And I made my own.

Then

I type in my username,
think up a password.

It comes to me quickly:

Inn0vAtiVeARts

FLYING THROUGH

Cyber school begins
and I speed through geometry.
All of it easier than I expected.

The other students must be behind too.

Log off, eat lunch.
Plug into chemistry.

Two whole units behind where we were
at Ketchum.
Still not simple,
but easier too, comparatively.

I soar—
      in the middle of chem, though,
      an email pops up on my phone.

Flight halted.

      Fiona.

      Is she angry that I stopped coming to class?
      Does she wonder what happened?

My own questions unnerve me.

I make sure to balance
all of the equations
before I
rest my wings,
check her words.

RISKS

Fiona says:
Mom called
asking to be refunded
for the second half
of the class.

Fiona assumes:
that she never knew
I was enrolled.
She says I'm very talented—
it's a shame
I couldn't be honest
but it seems like a complicated situation.

Fiona hopes:
I will get to take photography
in the future,
she would like to be able
to teach me
again.

I think:
of all the risks I took
to bring Fiona into my life.

I take:
my phone into the bathroom
where the drop-cam can't spy on me
and
thank her.

FASTER/SLOWER

When they get home
from work,

Dad & Mom & I
go over
    my schoolwork
    chores
    books I need from the library.

We make a plan for tomorrow.
Friday,
Mom's day off.

When I wake up,
log in,
I see Mom's not
    sleeping
    or cleaning
    or running errands
        like usual.

Today she is
            hovering
            over me
telling me to
do a problem faster/slower/better.

I tell her

I need to go to the library
for those books.
This time it's not a lie.

With her tired eyes
she says fine,
be back

in an hour or less.
Tells me she'll be timing me.

After this expulsion, any thread of trust—VANISHED.

WINGS

After the library,
books under my arm,
I don't wander
don't stop anywhere.

I make it home

<u>before</u> my time is up.

The bird engraved on our brownstone
lifts his wing,
     his own thumbs-up
at my return.

INTERLACED

Unlock the front door,
hang my key on the rack,
just like Mom always says to do.

I notice hers isn't there.

But her voice is.
Trembling, loud.
I step in, softly.

"How can you say that, David?
I've been trying to protect her—

she doesn't know. Never will."

I stand frozen,
rooted in place.

Startled now
by Dad,
angry, loud
back:

"She can feel it, Cynthia.
She's smart. She can <u>feel</u> it."

What does Holly feel?
        I wonder.
What does Mom think she doesn't know?

From the corner of my eye,
I see Mom's key on the floor,

golden, shining up at me.

"Just because she wasn't planned . . .
just because I didn't initially want her—
that I even thought of giving her away—
it doesn't mean
I don't love her now.
I don't know how you could even say something like that."

And in that moment
    I know
Mom's not talking about Holly.

VOICES FALL

I grip my library books tighter.

Just because she wasn't planned.

I was the one
who grew inside her.

Just because I didn't initially want her—

We were once
a part of each other.

Thought of giving her away—

Mom's words
ring loudly in my head
on a loop.

Everything buzzes,
dims.

What was Mom trying to protect me from?

Voices fall.
Muffled, crying.

I throw down my books.
Kick Mom's key under the table,

grab mine off the hook.
Slam the door.
Leave the way I came.

ALTERED

Digital photography
easily distorts reality.

With one click
an image is altered,

disguising the truth:

I was no marvelous surprise.
No happy accident.
No missing link.

Now I know the truth.
No more
filters.

I am really, and truly, alone.

ESCAPE

I have
to get far away from here.
Wonder: Who might be willing to go with me?

I text Silas:
Wanna escape?

He texts
back
quickly

        Always.

I don't wait to make a plan
        to pick a time and meeting place
just go downtown
directly to his school.

Surprise Silas.
Pick him up,
he'll take me
          away.
    Boston?
    Chicago?

Just the two of us
arm in arm
in another city's streets.

Another city's park.

Can hardly wait.

FLUORESCENCE

Scurry underground,
stuff myself into a crowded row of seats,
holiday tourists cramping an already-crowded space,
fluorescent lights glare at us,
everyone
squashed in
trying to breathe
in this city
of broken dreams.

Out of the subway,
I scurry back up
into the light,
my phone pings.

Notice my battery's low.

Ignore a text from Dad
asking where I am,
then a more frantic voice-mail message.

Follow the crowd.

Walk on.

JUXTAPOSITION

Park myself on a stoop
      wait for Silas
to get out of school.

Take a photo of a pigeon's beak
pecking some old gum.

     Remember Fiona's words on juxtaposition:

    How two different things
    brought into the same frame
    can work to emphasize their similarities
              and their differences.

Like me and Holly.

Her, adopted.
Me, unwanted.

I force the tears to stop,
         spot

     Silas's faded Icee-blue hair.
My heart   soars
but
his arm is around

some other girl—

and I know
     without getting any closer
it's the girl from the picture.

BEFORE THE LIGHT SHIFTS

Before I cross the street,
before the light shifts,

I can't help but watch—

as they stop walking

and

      kiss.

The whole street turns black and white.

Except them.

In full color, kissing.

ABERRATIONS

Walk up to Silas, tap him on the back.

> His image splits in two.

He motions for me to go away.

> A chromatic aberration.

His lips are locked, his back is turned
he doesn't know it's me.

A random person on the stairs says: "Damn, girl looks pissed."

> A lens defect. The colors don't bend as they should.

Silas turns, meets my eyes.
"Hey! What are you doing here?"

> Aberrations can be decreased by avoiding high-
> contrast conditions.

The girl wipes her mouth. Keeps hold of his hand.

> Purple rings float above her.

"Is this her?" she says like she knows who I am.

> Blue rings float above him.

He reaches his other hand to me.

> Silas comes back into focus.

SNAP & SCATTER

I take his arm and twist it.

Nearby branches snap from trees

        crack
        fall
        scatter.

He says
"Hey, stop, that hurts."

I say
"Hey, good"

before

I

let

go.

HISTORY IS ALL

"I thought we were exclusive—"

    "We are . . . she's . . . it's—
    we have history is all—"

History
is all?

As if history doesn't mean everything?

And suddenly I realize
we were never really together,
he never wanted an escape.
That was a lie.
              A dream.

We were never going to be like
    Ellery & Taryn
    Holly & Stefano.

I don't know what else to say
    so I just leave
    before he can see
the tears floating in my eyes.

How stupid I've been
<u>again</u>.

I start walking
and the city erupts
into a forest fire.

PERIPHERY

I half expect
     Silas
to   chase after
                         me
to at least call my name
tell me there's been a misunderstanding.
But—

     no one comes
     no one calls my name.

Flames flash
flicker
die.

Only soot remains.

If I misinterpreted
     why
my mom
never treated me
the way she treated Holly,

if I misinterpreted
     how
much Silas liked me,

how can I trust my

own interpretation

of   anything?

FOUNTAIN ANGEL

I walk for hours
all the way back uptown
until I find myself
in the park.

Bethesda Fountain.

Built in 1873,
soon after Seneca Village was destroyed.

In fifth grade,
when Mom declared my creativity
a "liability"

      room "too messy,"
      homework "too outside the box,"

Dad would take me here.

He called the statue a healing angel,
    said if I ran my fingers through the water,
      I'd get stronger, prove to Mom

I could do better.

Now,
fingertips in the angel's water,
I realize that
      no matter what

I never had a chance.

DIZZY

My whole life
Dad has been trying to prove to her
they didn't make a mistake:
      having me
      keeping me.

Questions
like

      Why didn't she want to have a child naturally?
      Why did she only want to adopt Holly?

dizzy me.
My stomach rumbles.

I buy a pretzel, take one bite

throw the rest
to the pigeons.

EXCAVATION

I walk on
through the park

       past twentysomethings talking about a movie,
       a homeless woman pushing a cart,
       a dog walker with five barking dogs

to Tanner's Spring.
Kneel.

Stick my hand into
the cold leaves and grass.

       Where there once was a village
                there is now a park.

       Maybe it's time for another excavation.

My own.

And then—

       when I look up—

I see her.

INTERSECTION

She
doesn't say anything
    (at first).

We stand and face each other

    (two tunnels running parallel).

We both reach out

    (converge).

GENEROSITY

"They're freaking out—
think you overheard something?"

> "I overheard Mom. She—
> Mom never wanted me—
> she even considered giving me up."

A long pause.

Then Holly says that must've felt terrible to overhear.

She looks around,
like she might find something else to say.
Scrunches her eyes together then opens them.
Says, "I'm not going to make excuses for them,
but I know they're really sorry."

When I don't say anything, she goes on.

"Linc, I know you're upset, but they want you
to come home . . .

I do too."

Says she knows it isn't always easy
      being her sister.
It isn't always easy
      being mine.

I know, I say.

"But you're my sister
no matter what,
you're my family."

My heart inflates, refills
the slightest bit.

OVERFLOWING

We sit for a while.
Holly asks me if I want to
hear something
that will take my mind off
everything else.

"Yes. *Please*."

She takes a deep breath.

   "I'm applying to a summer program in Ghana."

The wind picks up.

She thinks Mom & Dad will be mad,
won't let her go.

Won't understand.

I tell her I can relate.

Then, deep breath, "one for one,"

I tell her about IAA.

And as we share our secrets,

      an African American villager
      and an Irish one
      come together
         at this rushing stream
      to gather buckets of water.

SOMETIMES

It's cold,
but we stay outside a little longer,
sit on a bench.

I ask Holly
how she knew where to find me.
She said she walked
all the Seneca Village blocks

then remembered
how we used to play by the stream.
How we pretended
to fetch water.

I tell her then about Silas.
"I know I can be stupid
but I didn't think I was *that* stupid."

"Don't say that," she says.

"You're not stupid.
You just really liked him.

Sometimes when we like people,
we ignore the things about them
that we don't want to see."

She looks down then,
sad,
and I can't help but wonder
what more
she isn't telling me.

BACK THROUGH THE GATE

Eventually,
> we walk back.

> My   heart   speeds   up
> as we
> get closer

to home.

I tell her I don't want to see them,

I have nothing to say.

She says maybe they'll do the talking.

Almost all of me wants to keep walking,
go anywhere
except back there.

But Holly's hand holds firmly
to my own
as we walk through
the gate,

and we enter together.

IN/AWAY

"Oh, thank God," Mom says,
her eyes red.

They were about to head out
to look for me too.

She pulls me into a hug—
                    I pull away.

She lets me.

Dad says he's so relieved to see me.
Hugs me too.
But I shrug him off.
He guides Holly out of the room.

I want to yell at them not to go.
Not to leave me alone
         with her.

Mom sits on the couch.
Pats the seat beside her.

I sit as
far away
as I can.

     In the chair that no one ever sits in.

She looks sad, nods.

And then she starts talking.

FUNCTIONS

"Linc, I want to explain what I think you heard.

There's a lot you don't know about
my own childhood
because I haven't been ready to tell you.

There's something you asked about
when you were much younger
but I never really answered.

You asked why summers were happier without my father."

I look up.

This isn't the conversation
I expected.

"As you know, my father died before you and Holly were born.

But not much before.

In those last years, I hardly saw him.

That was a choice I made.

He was a violent man,
a terrible alcoholic.

Half the time he was out of his mind.

So—when Roy—"

Pause.
She clasps her hands together.
Exhales.

I feel my own heart rate pick up.
I have no idea what she's going to say.

  "Roy was an artist and he was also gay. Did you know that?

  It was something that my father tried to be okay with,
  sometimes.

  But really, he wasn't. Not on the inside.

  And when he drank, it was worse.

  He beat Roy, frequently.

  One night it got really bad.

  Broken bones.

  Called him horrible names.

  And Roy never fully recovered psychologically—

  Honey, he—"
And then she begins to cry.

"He committed suicide?"

I say it
so she doesn't have to.

She nods.

The air in the room

sits heavy.

> "If my father had been different,
> I know Roy would still be alive.
>
> He wrote in his note—"

Her voice cracks.
More tears fall.

> "He just wanted his approval, really.

> And Mom left Dad of course,
> finally.
> After."

Deep breath.

> "When I married your dad, I told him I never, ever

> wanted to pass on my dad's genes.

> Alcoholism runs in families, you know. And his was so
> severe."

Mom. Drinking now every Sunday.

> "And I have some issues of my own. Maybe you've noticed?"

I nod.

"I drank too, after everything.
Some things are tough to fight, and I guess I wanted to forget.

But then I stayed sober for a long time, sweetie.

All through med school, you and Holly being little—

so long—

I thought I could—"

"Drink just on Sundays."

She sighs.

"I thought I could handle it in moderation."

"So you didn't want to pass on his genes . . . or your own?"

"No I didn't, and it wasn't just that I—

I had so many fears thinking I could never be a good mom

considering the way I was raised.

But your dad wanted kids so badly

and when we went to Ghana, working with those orphans,

for the first time, I could picture myself as a mother.

So I told your dad we could look into adoption."

She pauses. Looks away from me.

"But then—as you know—

I got pregnant too—

and I was so scared about it.

Your dad really wanted you, Linc.

And, *yes*, I did think about putting you up for adoption.

But then—

you were born—"

She is weeping now.
I can't stop the tears
streaming down
my own cheeks
either.

"You looked so much like him."

"Your dad?"

"No, honey—
Roy.

So when I saw you
I knew I had to try.
To hold on.

Even if I was scared."

I wipe my face.

"And you were so creative
even as a child, just like Roy was.

But he struggled so much as an artist.
He never did well in school.
He flunked out of freshman year of college.
Tried to sell his art, never could—
he always needed money
which made Dad even more angry, disappointed—
he—

Roy never figured out how to find his way

in spite of Dad

like I did."

She pauses.

"Watching you struggle,

it's brought up a lot of my own past again.

But I thought if I wasn't hurting you the same way Dad hurt

Roy, I—

maybe—

but somehow—

in trying not to make the same mistakes my dad made,

I think a part of me has found the similarities anyway.

He would get mad at Roy
for failing, for drawing instead of studying.
He never took the time to try to help him
with his work.

So I've tried my hardest to be present
                    to help."

She lets out a sob.

Pulls herself back together.

"Linc, I know I haven't been easy on you, and maybe I should
have tried harder to listen to what it is you really want.
I know I need to work on myself. I'm trying.
I'm going to get back into therapy, to recovery.
Do better."

I look down.
"All *I've* ever wanted for you—and your sister—is for both of
you to not have to struggle.

To be able to function

                    to succeed

in this world."

The shadows of the window bars
crisscross on the floor.
In between them
light streams in
from lampposts
outside.

I try to process
everything I've just learned

this part of my past
        I never knew
that now feels like the opening
of a door.

So I say to Mom,
"Maybe I have my own way of functioning?
And succeeding?"

It sounds like a question
but I know it is an answer.

She looks at me,
nods.

The light from the lamppost
just barely
touches her shoulder.

TOUCH

After we sit
          breathe in silence
for a while

Dad comes in with tissues,
     gives me a sideways hug
     sits next to Mom.

Before leaving

I touch the place
on her shoulder

where the light hits.

LUCIDITY

That night
I dream:

I'm inside Gramercy Park.
I look down at my hands.
They are shadows.
Silas touches them
and
my shadow fingers
break
off

        one
        by
        one.

I shout for help.
Mom comes but says
she doesn't have the right medicine
to fix me.

She floats away.

I look down at a pigeon,
ask him if he has a key.
He shrugs and takes my picture.

EMPTY SPACE

I wake up early
     Saturday morning
but stay in bed,
hoping if I do
I can pretend

I dreamt it all—

    getting caught
        expelled
            jeopardizing my chances at IAA

        Silas and his ex
        Mom and her secrets

        me, unwanted,
        learning the truth.

I take pictures of the ceiling.

White
on white
on white.

GESTURES

Before her shift
Mom comes in
in her scrubs.

She has a breakfast tray.
Says I deserve something special.

She puts it down.
Then places a finger on Roy's camera.
Out on my desk.

> "I've been thinking,"
> she says,
> "if you think you can do photo class
> and keep up with your schoolwork ..."

She stops,
smiles.

"Really?"
I say,
then break into a smile back.

"Maybe for the next session?
In January?" I say.

> "Start fresh?" she asks.

"Start fresh," I confirm.

THE RIGHT MEDICINE

After she leaves my room
the details of my dream
come back into focus—
     Mom didn't have the right medicine.

I think of the truth—
     Roy so badly beaten.

Mom,
     an orthopedic surgeon,
Roy,
     robbed of his fight.

And I know
with startling clarity
that my family's
history may be in the choices
they—
we—
have all made

but our story
is still being written.

And

there's always room for

re-

vision.

WORDLESS

I eat Mom's pancakes
   check my texts

Ellery.

She said Holly texted her
a bunch last night
asking if she knew where I was.
She hopes I'm okay.

I text her that
I'm home, safe,
no need to worry.
I tell her sorry
for not listening to her
about Silas.
She was right.

Silas.

He sent a heart emoji.

He can't even say

sorry?

I toss the phone onto my bed.
Go find

Holly.

A SPACE FOR US

For the first time in a long time,
Holly & I have a lounge day in the den.

Pull out the couch,
make popcorn,
watch movie after movie.

Sometime later

we talk about my
conversation with Mom.
How intense
her childhood was.
How she makes
more sense to me now.

Holly says Mom talked to her too.
That she hopes things really will get better.

Then she says she has been feeling
more disconnected
from Stefano, Maggs
lately.

       Even from Mom.

That she keeps wanting to know more
about where she came from.

Feeling not quite there, not here either.

I say
sometimes it feels like what's
invisible
is more real than what's actually
in front of us.

As we sit,
        //side by side,
        knee to knee//

        we make a deal.
        To help each other,
        "one for one."

And—as we do—
I make a wish
that there was more room in this world
for those of us caught
in the space between.

REENTERING

I.
On Sunday,
just two weeks until winter break,
Dad comes in to help me plan
my cyber week.

We enter the cyber school website.
Notice there have been three comments made
about my post on *Richard III*.

Looks like you've already made some friends,
he says.

I raise my eyebrows,
then click in.

II.
Two days later,
Dad starts going back
to his office.

The days pass faster
than I expect.

The silence of the house
helps me think.

Seems like I have a lot in common
with these online kids.
Kicked out of schools.
Couldn't quite catch up.
Not sure where they belong.

III.

On Thursday,
a new comment
on the one I made about
Richard III's duplicity,
someone named Rachel
calls me insightful.

Later,
I hear from Silas.
It's been 5 days since he texted
          me a heart
       6 days since I saw him
           with that other girl.
Now he wants to see me.

I ask him if he's still with *her*.

He tells me I don't understand.
That they're old friends, will always be.

The first day we met
I was so drawn to him.
We seemed so similar.

I almost say: let's meet up.

But I stop.
We are our choices.
And I know that
      I don't trust him.

My stomach knots
then releases

I think of finally standing up for myself
to Mom.
It feels the same when I write Silas back.
I tell him it's over.

Deep breath in and then I write:
    I'm not okay being in your peripheral view.
    I know now I'm worth someone's full focus.

I tell him it's over
then take a celebratory selfie.
It's me: I'm smiling, centered.

Then, to the class,
I write about the pity I feel
for Richard III.

When someone likes my comment,
calls it intelligent,

      my body feels lit,
      and this time
      it's from within.

ARRIVAL

      I take a break

      get a snack.

Look to see if the mail has arrived.

      And there it is.

An envelope from the

      Innovative Arts Academy

with my name.

I don't wait.
I tear it open.

BUT/AND/THEN

Your portfolio is remarkable . . . strong vision and voice . . .
Highly recommended by your teacher . . .

But then:

When we called the school for your transcript we were made aware of
your expulsion . . . and your current 2.4 GPA.

We regret to inform you that
we cannot offer you a spot . . .

Underneath my feet,
the ground cracks.

Eyes tear.
Blink them away to see
below that:

Please consider applying again once you strengthen your GPA at
your current school. We offer midyear placement on a case-by-case
basis. We hope to see more from you in the future.

Keep creating!

QUICKSAND

I run
to my room
tear up
the schedule I made

a scrap falls to the floor:

Sept: Go to IAA for junior year!!

I was moving forward
            finally on a path

but—now—

I am spun around,

                directionless

                        lost.

The ground is quicksand
and I sink.

SEE BEYOND

If only
    I hadn't made some of the choices I did
    maybe the letter would say

        congratulations.

Maybe
    the letter would say
    I was headed
    to a place where I belong.

My mind-camera
    reconfigures the words:

We can offer you a spot . . .

I fold my letter
into a paper airplane.

Crease by crease.
Covering the words of rejection.

Watch it zip around my room.

For a moment I
see it speed up

    but then—

    my imagination fails and
    it falls.

THE GOOD PARTS

I lie there for I don't know
how long.

But after a while,
I hear Holly's voice
in my head
telling me
I'm not stupid.
I hear her
telling me

to get up off the floor.

Grab my letter,
take it to the park,
where Holly practices.

I call to her,
        doing drills before her last game.

She looks at me in surprise,
        says something to her coach,
        jogs to meet me.

What happened, she asks
right away.
I show her the letter from IAA.

She says she knows I'm upset,
but I need to focus on the good parts:

"They loved your photographs!
They want you to apply again!"

She says I'll get my grades up.
We'll make a plan together.
Things are going to be okay, I'll see.

We walk as the stones
skitter under our feet.
Then she changes the subject,
says
she believes me about Stefano.

The leafless trees stop in the wind,
lean their branches in

to listen.

TURN OFF

She says losing her virginity
made her think more
about her birth mother.

How scary it would be
to get pregnant
at our age.

How she feels like
she can barely take care
of herself sometimes.
How it all made her pull away
from Stefano.

How he got mad,
how it turned her off.

How he said things she was surprised to hear.

Made her realize
I wasn't lying.

He said he wants to be with her.
She said she has lots to think about.

And for the first time
in a long time
I know
she won't choose Stefano
over me.

PARTS OF OURSELVES

Holly says he's here,
watching in the stands,
but she's pretending not to
see him.

As we talk,
I realize—
Holly & I
are both good at pretending.
Not always showing the truth.
Wonder if maybe we learned to be that way.

As we walk,
an older white woman
passes by.

Looks at us.

Instinctively,
we lock hands.

"We're twins!" I yell out.
And Holly laughs.

The woman looks away.

Maybe we've both been hiding
parts of ourselves,
so tired of being watched,
              being judged.

I think of Holly years ago

on our trip to Ghana.
How badly she wanted to fit in.

How hard
       it has been to be her.
How much
       I never realized.

"You know, I always wanted to match you."
She smiles, says,
"I know."

And then:

"But maybe
even if we don't match,
we still belong together."

And the leafless branches
wind together tighter,
bend toward us,
bow,
whisper:

Maybe a family isn't something you're born into
as much as it is

something you choose
to be a part of

every day.

Holly & I squeeze hands.

Holly & I

deciding each day
to be sisters

deciding each day
to fight for each other.

To grab hands and
hold on.

BETTER THAN

We walk back to the field.

I hold on to my letter,
keep my mind's eye
on the good parts
     like Holly said,
watch her play soccer

and think

it's not that my sister's life is perfect

it's more that she is brave.

MAKE A WISH

Saturday,
Christmas music
floating through the house,
Holly's in her room
at her computer.

I walk in.

Her hair is natural.
Soft, curly.
I haven't seen it this way in years.

"Your hair looks nice."

She touches it.
   "You think? I might grow it out. Or maybe cut it short.
   Better for sports anyway."

She waves me over.
Shows me the images:

   Students drumming together.
   A classroom with Twi written on the blackboard.
   Students pounding fufuo.

"Remember doing that?" she grins.

   "Yeah! Of course."

I see tears mist in her eyes,
despite her smile.

"You ready?"
I ask.

"Almost," she says.

    "So,
    tomorrow night then?"

She's nervous,
    I can tell,
but her eyes go soft,
and agree.

That night,
I draw two big, green
four-leaf clovers
on my wall.

One for Holly,
one for me.

I take a picture of it
and send it to her.

I caption the image in my mind:
This is going to work.

WHERE THE LIGHT PASSES THROUGH

Sunday, lights twinkling on the tree,
no wineglasses present,
Mom, Dad & Holly do the crossword,
ask if I want to help.

I edit photos mostly
but when Mom says:

> "The word for 'a space through which light passes'"

I know when I say
"aperture"
that I have gotten it right.

ALL AT ONCE

We made a deal
to help each other.
That night,
we enact our plan.

First step
(deep breath):
my turn.

Confess:
"I needed photo class for something else.
Something bigger.
I forged your signatures,
applied to IAA.
Used Dad's checkbook.
I did try harder to do better
                to get my grades up,
just not for the reason
you thought."

Tell them I know I would
make them proud
if I could get into IAA.
Especially now,
because of cyber school,
where I'm actually doing well,
I have a real shot at getting in.

Holly says:
"It really seems like it would be
a great place for her."

Before they can say anything,
I show them the rejection letter.

"I want to reapply for spring
of junior year.
With your support this time.
You don't have to answer me now,
just promise me you'll think about it.
Please."

They turn to each other,
then to me,
nod.

And then: Holly's turn.

LETTING IT OUT

She explains that there's an amazing
academic opportunity available to her,
she thinks she can get a scholarship,
                    go for free.

A study abroad program
for a month this summer.

"That sounds exciting!" Dad says.

"Where is it?" Mom asks.

Inhale up,
exhale down.

"Ghana."

SIMULTANEOUSLY

Holly says she appreciates the time we went together.
But now she wants to immerse herself in the culture,
get a better sense of it.

"Plus, it will look good to colleges,"
she adds quickly.

Mom and Dad look at each other.

And then I say, "I could go with her."

They turn their focus on me, confused.

"Why would you want to go?" Mom asks.

I hold up my letter again.

"If I am going to reapply to IAA,
I'll need a new body of work to show.
Remember how we went to Aburi, the mountain town?
Remember that outdoor sculpture museum?
The rain forest?
Think of how many amazing photographs I could get . . ."

Mom looks worried.
Dad is the one to speak:
        "Okay. Well, we have a lot to talk about.
        Without you girls."
They try to hold steady
while Holly & I
hope.

COMPOSITION II

Her knee is shaking
as she sits at her desk.
I can feel her nerves.

"I'm scared too,"
I say.
But it's the good kind of scared.

I distract Holly.
We decide to go out for ice cream.
A distraction.

I watch our stride fall in line,
two leaves almost touching.

Can't help but notice that
                    the composition of a relationship
            changes

as we change individually.

The spaces between us

at any moment
might   **widen**,
then   narrow,

but for this sweet moment,
with a gentle push of the wind,
Holly & I

            have found a place of //overlap.//

SHIMMERS

The next day,

I tell my parents I'm going
        to see Ellery
and I don't have to lie.

I leave
feeling

light and   free.

Ellery hugs me,
says how much she misses me
at school.
I tell her how cyber school
is actually okay.
Tell her about IAA rejection,
        about Holly,
                our plan,
                        Roy,
                        Mom,
all of it.
She can't believe how much is going on in my life.
While we talk, Taryn FaceTimes.
I tell Ellery,
        "It's okay, pick up."

I apologize to Taryn
for Silas being a jerk a while back.
She says she's sorry I was expelled.
"Maybe we can try hanging out again sometime.

Without him."
        "For sure."
Ellery tells Taryn she'll call her back later.

Then she turns to me and says:
"She told me she's in love with me . . . and I told her me too."

I wait for jealousy
to find its way under my skin.
But it doesn't.

Instead:

"I'm happy for you, El," I say.

        "Thanks!
        You and Holly's plan? I think it's gonna work,"
        she grins.

Then
the fairy on Ellery's shirt
comes alive,
shimmers
flies to me

whispers
that she agrees.

The words light me up

and I can feel myself glow.

PROMISE

On the subway,
I think of Mom,
wonder if she and Roy
ever made deals

like me and Holly.

Back home,
I dare myself.

Open the closet.

Take out the box.

Knock on her door.

"Mom?"

Reading,
her knees up
almost like a child.

"Could you tell me more about him?"

I walk to her bed.
Sit down.

She opens the box.

And,
memory by memory,

383

tears in between,

Mom tells me about
     Roy's favorite song
     his drawings
     his boyfriend.

As she talks
I press a promise into my heart:
one day,
through my art,
I will honor him.

GIFTS

Christmas comes.
Mom & Dad
sit us down.

They've made their decision.

"Linc, you first."

They say I did a lot of lying, a lot of stealing.
They do not approve of any of it.

But they understand how badly I want this,
that I deserve the chance to go
                after what I want
      deserve the chance to
earn their trust again.

I may apply for spring semester of junior year.

          The windows open themselves.

"Thank you!
Thank you!
Thank you!"

          The sun streams in,
          I swallow it hot, full.

Give them each a hug.

Then, with a glance at my sister,
I ask, "What about Holly?"

SOMEDAY

Holly may apply to her program too.

But—Mom and Dad will join us.
Instead of Ireland,
they will accompany us to Ghana.
I will stay with them and their doctor friends.

That way Holly can have her own experience,
but we can still see her.
They can take me to the best places
for photography.

And then, on the way back,
we could stop in Ireland.

Take pictures there too.
It's a bit of a compromise,
and more time with my parents
than I would have liked.
But it's still a good offer
so it's not difficult to say, "Okay, deal."

Holly thanks them too.
Says she promises it'll help with her college essay someday.

Mom shakes her head and says,
"Let's just hope it helps Holly be Holly.
Whoever that is."

We each wipe tears away
as the house
sighs in relief.

THIS MOMENT NOW

After our talk,
Mom asks
to look at my history photos.
I show her everything:

     The playground,
          the church,
               the stream,
                    the leaves.

The one of the two girls skipping
she calls "breathtaking."

Then suggests we all go for a Christmas walk
in the park.

As we climb Summit Rock,
     also called Nanny Goat Hill
        for the goats that used to be here
        before the Park was a park,
I realize how different this trip is
from the last time I was here
     with Silas.

But I don't focus on
the way he betrayed me.

I click past that
to all the ways
        the moments with him
        all the choices I made

even if they weren't always the right thing
led me to this moment

scampering
summiting
with my family.

We all gather together,
I take our picture.

And the shot is perfect.

ONE LAST FRAME

HIGH UP, HOLDING

Two girls in
Kakum National Park, Ghana.
Canopy walk through
the rain forest.
One at a time.
In a line.
Taking turns
leading
and following.
High up.
Holding the ropes.
Parents down below
waving.
Two sisters above
laughing

soaring

yelping

swinging free.

                Linc & Holly
                Holly & Linc

suspended
by trees

and light.

ACKNOWLEDGMENTS

This story has been a shape-shifter.

Thank you to Sara Crowe for believing in it ever since its first form. And then advocating for it through every metamorphosis.

A million thank-yous to Liza Kaplan for being a word sculptor and giving this story the shape that fit it best. Linc became a braver character because of you. And I became a braver writer. Thank you to the entire Philomel/Penguin Young Readers team for all the work you do to birth books. Thank you specifically to Talia Benamy, Michael Green, Kristin Boyle, Jenny Chung, Nicole Wayland, Laurel Robinson and Kaitlyn Kneafsey for all their time, effort and dedication. You are all magicians. I appreciate you.

Thank you to my photographer mother, Mariette Pathy Allen, who taught me to play and experiment in invisible worlds. And then make them visible. Thank you also for being an expert reader.

Thank you to Sarah Zwerling, photographer extraordinaire, for graciously reading the book and providing feedback.

Thank you to Sarah Hannah Gómez and Dhonielle Clayton for being sensitivity readers. I am humbled by all your suggestions, and I cannot thank either of you enough. Thank you for being willing to teach me.

Thank you to Linda Washington for reading early on and giving me some invaluable feedback.

Laurie Morrison, thank you for reading this a few times and giving me all your expert advice. You are one of the smartest people I have ever met.

Laura Sibson, thank you also for reading and for your loyal, true friendship.

Immense thanks to Diana Wall of the Seneca Village Project for being an expert reader. I would never have known about the park's incredible history if it hadn't been for your work. For more on their project, see: http://www.mcah.columbia.edu/seneca_village/.

Thank you to the Central Park Conservancy for their information on Seneca Village as well.

I am thankful for the time I spent in Ghana many years ago, for the families that showed me love and warmth and for the friends I made there.

To my Philly community, thanks to so many of you for always asking so much about my writing and for being incredibly supportive and thoughtful friends to me and my whole family.

Thank you to my own sister, Julia; our relationship has fluctuated in closeness and distance, but the love and devotion has never changed. Being a sister is one of my favorite things to be.

Thank you to Jon, Tate and Lily, who listen to me talk about my story ideas and about my days of writing with kind eyes, supportive ears and open hearts. Every day, I am grateful to be a member of our family.